GIFT OF

John Warren Stewig

Carthage

D0966499

A DAY FOR VINCENT CHIN AND ME

HEDBERG LIBRARY
CARTHAGE COLLEGE
KENOSHA, WISCONSIN

Cur
PZ
7
B22593
Day
2001

A DAY FOR
VINCENT
CHIN ᴬᴺᴰ ME

Jacqueline Turner Banks

Houghton Mifflin Company
Boston 2001

Copyright © 2001 by Jacqueline Turner Banks

All rights reserved. For information about permission to reproduce selections from this book, write to Permissions, Houghton Mifflin Company, 215 Park Avenue South, New York, New York 10003.

www.houghtonmifflinbooks.com

The text of this book is set in 12-point Berkeley Book.

Library of Congress Cataloging-in-Publication Data
Banks, Jacqueline Turner.
A day for Vincent Chin and me / by Jacqueline Turner Banks.
p. cm.
Summary: Although Tommy, a Japanese-American sixth-grader, has serious doubts when his mother starts organizing a rally to fight racism, once he and his friends find a cause of their own he gains more understanding of her motives.
ISBN 0-618-13199-X
[1. Racism—Fiction. 2. Social action—Fiction. 3. Schools—Fiction. 4. Japanese Americans—Fiction. 5. Prejudices—Fiction.] I. Title.
PZ7.B22593 Day 2001   [Fic]—dc21   00-054158

Manufactured in the United States of America
QUM   10   9   8   7   6   5   4   3   2   1

In memory of my first advocate, my father
Jackson Otis Turner
June 9, 1918–February 6, 1996

Thank you, Daddy, for teaching us that it's not enough
to care: we have to be willing to fight for our causes.

To Tom Joyner, Tavis Smiley, Sybil Wilkes, J. Anthony
Browne, and the rest of the Tom Joyner Morning
Show crew for demonstrating the power of advocacy
to a new generation.

Always my family, Reggie, Regina, Geoffrey, and Jeremy
for your patience, respect, and love.
To my "triplet" Rasheed A. Vanzant for your valuable
reading and comments.

All of you make it work; any mistakes are my own.

CHAPTER ONE

It's unusual to see my parents talking to each other when the sun is still out. I'm not calling them vampires, or anything like that. They ask each other questions and they talk to us, to me and my little sister, Quinn, but I don't think of them as having long conversations until after we're all in bed.

My room is between theirs and Quinn's, and some nights, when I don't go right to sleep, I can hear my father's low, muffled voice. I can't hear my mother's voice, but I assume he's not in there talking to himself. It's not often that I know or care what they're saying to each other, but on the day it all began, I knew.

As my friend Jury would say, "Stories are best heard from the beginning," so that's where I'll start.

I was on my way home from school. It was a great day. The sun was shining and the wind wasn't blowing. This meant that, for the first time in three days, my eyes weren't burning. I have allergies. My father's a doctor, and I know exactly what I'm allergic to, but listing everything here would be too embarrassing. I'll just say I'm not allergic to the sun. Everything else associated with spring is suspect.

As I was walking down my block, I was thinking about the conversation I'd just had with my friends, Judge and Jury Jenkins, Angela Collins, and Faye Benneck. The twins, the girls, and I had been talking about current movies. When Jury described one film as a "chick flick," Faye freaked. Her actual words were, "You're a sexist pig, Jury Jenkins!"

You'd have to know Jury to know that Faye wasn't going to get away with that. Jury's a twin, and most people can't even get away with calling him by his brother's name. Jury always evens the score. He smiled, and I knew he was getting ready to deliver one of his ridiculous sayings.

"The man who has eaten his field will call the hungry man greedy," Jury said.

We were a half block from Faye's turnoff. Everybody stopped walking and looked at him. For the past three or four years, Jury has collected clichés. Lately he's been branching out to proverbs, mostly African, but some Chinese too. At first we were glad he was moving away from clichés— but then his proverbs started to become more and more confusing.

"What's that suppose to mean?" Faye asked.

"Think about it," Jury answered while giving her an

all-knowing grin. Which meant that he didn't have a clue either.

Angela, frustrated, started to say something, then stopped, balled up her fist, and hit Jury's left arm—hard. It was so unexpected, coming from her, that Judge and I started laughing.

"I can't believe I did that! See what you made me do, Ju-ry?" Angela said. (Both Faye and Angela tend to break Jury's name into two parts when they're trying to make a point.) It might have been her way of apologizing, but she still looked angry enough to hit him again.

"Yeah, right, I made *nonviolent*—you hit me!"

Angela was looking at us—me, Judge, and Faye—with pleading eyes. "I just get so sick of his random sayings. Do you know what it's like to have to listen to that foolishness day after day?"

Apparently, she had forgotten that she was talking to three people who *were* listening to it day after day.

"At least you don't have to *live* with him," Judge said.

Jury had something to say about that too, but I was at my turnoff and I knew that if it was worth repeating, Angela would tell me the next day in class or one of them would call me. We're close like that; all five of us have been best friends since kindergarten. We call ourselves the Posse, but we haven't had much success getting anybody else to call us that.

I was walking down my street, still cracking up about

Angela socking Jury and thankful for the clean air. I was wondering if the rain we had the night before was responsible—and then I heard it. I heard my sister scream.

My mother says that when we were babies, she could identify my and Quinn's cries in a room full of wailing babies. I'm like that about my little sister. I'm not saying it has anything to do with my great love for her, although, as little sisters go, she's all right. But her cry is horrible! The pitch is so high, the neighborhood dogs and I are probably the only living creatures who can hear its initial screech.

"Tom-*meee*! Tom-*meee*, help!" she called out while jumping up and down and pointing down the road. I glanced behind me. Up the slight hill, a car was stopped at the stop sign. My street is long and especially hilly. It's laid out like a roller coaster, which makes it great for skateboarding, but bad for pedestrians. The car was a small yellow sporty thing with two of those flip-top type headlights. Standing on one of the street's crests, I could see the car's shiny front grille. It looked like an animal, maybe a lion, getting ready to pounce—but on what? I looked back at my sister, who was also on a peak. That was when I noticed something moving between me and Quinn in the road below me. I could make out the beach ball, but it took me a moment to focus in on my sister's friend Latecia. She was in the center of the road and squatted over the ball like she was smelling it or something weird like that. Maybe she was blowing more air into it. I didn't have time to think about it until later, but I have to give Quinn a lot of credit. She was able to see what was about to happen and think of a "solution" in a time frame that worked. I'm a gifted student and I know I'm intelligent, but when Quinn does something smart, I've caught my mother and father glancing at each other. She's a really smart kid. I think they think I'll resent it if they compare us or something like that, but I'm smart enough to know that Quinn is leaps ahead of where I was at her age. I'm proud of her.

From about three o'clock until five-thirty, our street is like a combination of the Indianapolis Speedway and a wild roller-coaster ride. Drivers love to race down my street. What Quinn had figured out is that the driver of the yellow car, and most of the other drivers coming from the college and the downtown area, know that that stop sign is the last one until they hit the highway. The most important thing my little sister had figured out was that, even if the after-work speed-racer spotted Latecia in time to blow his horn like crazy, Latecia might not hear it—she's deaf. Even with the help of hearing aids in both ears, she misses a lot.

Like I said, I didn't have time to think about what to do. I ran down the middle of the street, hopeful that the driver would be able to see me. I heard the car picking up speed and knew that by the time the driver saw Latecia, it would be too late. Latecia was still facing Quinn, her back to me.

Slowly standing up, she raised the ball over her head, ready to throw it back to Quinn.

She never got the chance.

As I grabbed her, the ball dropped out of her hands. I could hear the screeching of brakes as the two of us fell on the grass in front of Mr. Bickle's house. When I looked back at the street, the car rolled over the beach ball as the car came to an abrupt stop. The ball made a loud popping noise. Latecia started crying.

Mrs. Jones must know her daughter's cry too—when I looked up, I was surprised to see her standing next to us. It was hard to tell how much time had passed. I followed Mrs. Jones's shocked gaze to the street. I could smell the burning rubber. The driver looked at us with a confused expression. He was inches from where Latecia had been. I got the feeling that he knew something had happened, but he wasn't sure what. Instead of getting out of the car, he shrugged his shoulders and then sped off. Mrs. Jones must be stronger than she looks, because the next thing I knew, she had scooped me and Latecia up off the grass. "What do I have to do to stop these idiots?" she said as she hugged us both close.

I pulled away. "I don't know, Mrs. Jones."

"It took the city over a year to put up the 'deaf child in neighborhood' signs, not that anybody bothers to read them." She was looking at the flat beach ball and talking in that way adults do that makes you think they're talking to themselves. When she looked back at me, her body jerked as if she just remembered that I was there. "Oh Tommy, thank you. Thank you so much. That flat ball out there could have been my baby."

Her "baby" was still crying and I'm not good with crying kids. I mumbled "No problem," and started toward my sister and home.

"What else do we have to do?" Mrs. Jones asked as she stepped into the street to pick up the useless ball.

What had happened with Latecia must have frightened Quinn; she was a little clingy for the next hour or so. But by the time our mother got home, about two hours later, things were back to normal.

At dinner that evening, Quinn started to tell our mother what had happened.

"I know all about it, sweetie. I spoke to Brenda Jones on the phone earlier."

It's a rare day that my mother will stop Quinn from telling one of her long, well-detailed stories. Dinnertime was a big deal in her home when she was growing up, and she wants it to be for us too. If my dad hadn't worked late at the hospital, he'd be there too—ready to share his day's events.

"Tommy, I'm really proud of you. Brenda said you might have saved Latecia's life."

I shrugged my shoulders. What's a guy supposed to say to that?

"There's something I need to tell you," my mother continued. "I know you've noticed how busy I've been lately with my group. We've linked with some other groups around the state and, two weeks from Saturday, we're planning a march on the state capitol."

"What kind of march?" Quinn asked.

"We're calling it A Day for Vincent Chin."

"Who's he?" I asked.

CHAPTER TWO

"Actually it's who *was* Vincent Chin," my mother said.

"Okay, Mom, who *was* he?"

"In the early eighties, the American automobile industry was going through some hard times. There were massive layoffs and plant closings at a time when Japanese cars were selling very well in this country. Chin was a young man who lived in Detroit. You know that they call Detroit 'Motor City' because of all the car factories there?"

Quinn nodded, but I think my mother meant it as a rhetorical question. My mother's tone changed, and I didn't like the seriousness that I heard in her voice. I decided it was time to zone out on them. Chilling, I consider it one of my finer skills.

"On June nineteenth, 1982, Vincent Chin was in a Detroit bar with some of his friends. They were celebrating Vincent's good news."

"What news?" Quinn asked.

Chilling wasn't working for me. How could it with Quinn asking all those questions?

"He was getting married soon, and his friends were there after work toasting him," my mother explained. "Apparently, there were some auto workers in the bar. They saw Vincent's group and went over and started blaming them for Detroit's economic problems."

"Why?" Quinn asked.

There is such a thing as too much curiosity. Why couldn't that brainy child see where this was going? I really didn't want to hear it. I tried singing a rap in my mind but I had to admit, it didn't work.

"These men blamed the Japanese and the Japanese automobile industry for the problems Detroit was having," my mother said.

Okay, the story had hit a snag. "Didn't you say his name was Chin?" I asked. Being Japanese Americans ourselves, we all knew that Chin was not a Japanese name.

"That's right, dear, his name was Vincent Chin, he was Chinese American, but the men thought Vincent and his friends were Japanese. Or maybe their racism prevented them from understanding the difference. They were all Detroiters and unemployment was a Detroit problem. They had all been drinking and that certainly didn't help matters.

"When Vincent's party was over and he went outside to

his car, two of the men were waiting for him—a forty-five-year-old man and his twenty-five-year-old stepson."

I didn't want my mother to continue. I could tell by the look on her face and the tone of her voice that it was going to be something terrible. I wished I hadn't started listening in the first place.

"Two days before his wedding, they beat Vincent Chin to death with baseball bats. He was twenty-seven years old."

I tried not to look at Quinn. My sister is at that age where sad things make her cry. Sometimes her crying will make me sad too—but that's not to say that I cry when she does.

"Mom, that's so awful. What did his girlfriend do?" Quinn asked.

I could hear the tears in her voice and forced myself not to look at her.

"Honey, I don't know what happened to his fiancée. And, yes, it is an awful story. I didn't tell you about it to make you sad. I just wanted both of you to understand how important this rally is. We must never forget the Vincent Chin story. We can't let America forget Vincent Chin."

"Why?"

My mother sighed before she answered Quinn. "It's important that every human being is treated with respect. It doesn't matter that he wasn't of Japanese descent, that's not the point of the story. Even if he'd been Japanese American, he wouldn't have deserved to die. *He* wasn't the problem. The problems Detroit and the rest of the country were having with Japanese imports were as much my concern as a Japanese American as they were the concern of Irish Americans or African Americans, because we're *all* Americans."

"Then why do we need to put another country in front of 'American'? And why do we need a special day to draw attention to ourselves?" I asked.

"Tommy, I know that fitting in is important at your age..."

It wouldn't have mattered what she said next. I hate it when adults say something like that. It's like they're saying, what you're feeling now isn't important because when you grow up you'll feel differently.

As we finished dinner, my mother told us about all the plans her group had made for the rally and all the support they were getting from college students around the state. One of the reasons they had scheduled the event for April instead of June, when Chin was killed, was so that the college students could participate.

She seemed happy talking about it. I can't say I was paying that much attention. My mother loves to get involved in her little projects. I wasn't too concerned until she remarked, "I probably need to warn you. There's some people around who don't want to see this happen. They could create problems for us."

"Who?" I asked.

"I don't know their names, but men who feel like the ones who killed Vincent Chin."

"They want to kill you, Mommy?" Quinn asked. Her fearful expression would have made you think the bad men were at the door.

"No, she means there will be some protesters at her rally."

"It could be a little more than that, Tommy. You see, I'm the spokesperson for the rally."

"Here in Plank," I added, thinking my mother needed clarification.

"No, across the state."

A hundred thoughts crossed my mind and, to be honest, not many of them had to do with my mother's safety. I felt sick to my stomach, the way I do when I take my strongest allergy pill. "Are you saying that you could be on television talking about this?"

"Yes," she answered. "Actually we have several interviews already scheduled."

I don't know what I was thinking when she first started telling us about this rally. I guess I figured it wouldn't involve me any more than her bake sales at the community center or her volunteer work at the hospital, but now I knew better. She was getting ready to go public and undo twelve years of my hard work. For as long as I've been in school, I've tried to be just one of the guys, not Tommy the smart kid with glasses, not Tommy the doctor's son—and certainly not Tommy the Japanese kid!

My own mother was planning to go on television and proclaim to the world that not only were we one of about twenty-five Asian families in Plank, Kentucky, but that we were *Japanese Americans with Attitude.*

CHAPTER THREE

The next morning my eyes popped open before the sun had finished rising. My friends are a very opinionated bunch. I can't remember now if it was Faye or Angela, but about a month ago one of them said she wanted a job that wouldn't require her to get up before she woke up on her own. Jury told her she'd better get a job testing mattresses. He was trying to be funny, as usual, and as usual Judge took him seriously, saying, "She'd still have to get up and go to work at a certain time."

Until that conversation I never thought about the fact that I rarely get a chance to sleep until my eyes open on their own. I have no idea what my natural body clock wake-up time is. I do know that if I sleep too long, I get a slight headache.

I was thinking about all of this that next morning to avoid thinking about the dream that had forced me straight up in the bed. Maybe I should call it a nightmare. The first thing I remembered was the flat ball in the middle of the street, only it wasn't a ball, it was Latecia's face. Mrs. Jones came running out of the house. She started screaming. The next thing I knew, my mother was out there. A crowd had gathered, but somehow they thought that my mother had done something to flatten Latecia. They pulled baseball bats out of nowhere and started beating her. I tried to block the hits, but they kept pushing me away. I tried to tell them that she was innocent, that she didn't do anything to Latecia. They didn't stop. I ended up behind the crowd, watching as their arms rose and fell, beating down my mother.

Just before her last scream woke me, I noticed that the back of the necks of the men beating my mother were so red, they looked like they'd been painted with blood.

My heartbeat was so loud, if anybody else had been in my room they would've heard it. I know how in a weird way dreams can show you things that affected you during the day, so I understood where the nightmare came from. But the image of the red necks was very upsetting. I've heard the term *redneck* my whole life; it's always bothered me. My family and the people I know don't use words like that, but I've heard kids at school use it to describe other kids. One kid I know wears a T-shirt that reads, "Redneck and Proud of It." It bothered me that, on some level, I must be the kind of person who would use an expression like that.

I couldn't remember the last time I was so scared. It had to have been when I was a kid. The thought of trying to go back to sleep didn't cross my mind. I sat down at my computer and answered some E-mail. I have pen pals all over the world. I tried very hard not to think about the dream, but it was still on my mind two hours later when I got to school.

My first class in the morning is my GATE class. GATE is a class for the gifted and talented—whatever that means. I shouldn't say that, I know what it means. It means I don't have to study a lot for most tests and my reward is an extra class each day—go figure. Faye and Angela are in the class too. Our GATE teacher is what they call innovative, which pretty much means she comes up with goofy stuff for us to do. For the past two days we've been studying perception, the way different people look at things. Some of it was kind of cool, like when she showed us one picture and some kids saw a monster and other kids saw a pretty woman looking in a mirror. She also has a picture of a vase that, when you look closely, is actually two people facing each other. That morning, there were papers on all twenty desks. I glanced at mine before the bell rang. The title was, "Build a Person."

I needed to talk to the Posse. Faye was sitting down reading the paper. That's Faye for you—the second bell hadn't rung and she was over there trying to get the jump on the rest of us. Faye and Angela are the most competitive people I know and will probably ever know. I caught Angela walking in the door. She was smiling that smile of hers; something or *someone* was on her mind.

I think Angela is one of the prettiest girls in the school, but I would never tell that to a soul. Thoughts like that can really mess up a friendship. It's too bad too, because I've got a feeling Angela needs to hear that she's pretty. It's not that she has a self-esteem problem—she truly believes she's one of the smartest people (teachers included) in the school—but I know that looks are important to girls, and since she's not a blue-eyed blonde, nobody makes a fuss over Angela.

Earlier this year, Faye developed a crush on Jury and it almost destroyed the old group. I shuddered while thinking of that time and was determined not to let the same thing happen between Angela and me.

But Angela was the one I needed to talk to now. I beckoned for her to come over, even as I started walking in her direction. Angela doesn't like to be told to do anything, and even a friend asking her to walk across the room is subject to annoy her.

"Isn't it a wonderful day, Tommy?" she asked, still smiling her mysterious smile.

"It's okay. I'm not sneezing. Angela, I need your advice."

"My *sage* advice."

"Okay, I need your sage advice." Angela's vocabulary tested at 12.5 on a test we took a few months back. That means she can use and understand words like a student in the fifth month of the twelfth grade. She never lets us forget it. Faye and I tested in the end of the eleventh-grade range, but like I said, I hang with some very competitive girls.

"How can I help you, dear, sweet Tommy?"

That stopped me. She's never said anything like that before. Her mood would bear watching, but first things first. "Look, girl, if you're in love or something, please do us all a favor and keep it to yourself. Especially if it involves anybody in the Posse."

"Dear, sweet, wonderful, albeit misguided, Tommy." She touched my shoulder, like an adult might. "What can I do for you?"

"Remember last year when we were selling that candy in the mall and we talked about race?"

"As you know, my memory is excellent, so I'll assume your question is rhetorical. Continue."

"My mother is getting ready to do something that could get her in trouble and destroy my life. I can't deal with it, I need—" What I really needed was more time, since right at that moment, the last bell rang. Angela's goofy expression had grown serious—I could see I'd caught her attention.

"The teacher is having us work in groups today. Can you tell me about it if we work together?" she asked.

"Maybe. Depends on who's in the group."

As it turned out, Angela was in my group but so were Faye and Jeff Sewell. I wouldn't have minded Faye hearing what I had to say, but I don't know Jeff that well. I didn't get to bring up my problem again until the teacher announced that it was time to start putting the room back in order.

"Finish what you were saying," Angela said, standing next to me as she held the back of her chair. I took the chair from her and started to return it to her row.

"It's about this rally my mother's planning."

She had a pencil in her mouth and her theme book under her chin. She was rummaging through her backpack for something. "The Vincent Chin march?" she asked, although it sounded more like "Duh Benson Fin marf?" through her mouthful of pencil.

"You know about it?"

She dropped the pencil in her bag. I don't know what she'd been searching for but she didn't find it. "Sure, the Deltas, my mother's sorority, are going to march."

"How do you feel about it?" I was talking to her back. She dropped her bag onto her chair, then she turned around and watched me put my chair back in my row.

"I think it's cool. Very sixties. Why, have you got a problem with it?"

Angela's enthusiasm about the march made me hesitate. "I don't know. Maybe. But there's something else on my mind. I'm going to need the Posse's help."

CHAPTER FOUR

The twins were waiting outside for us. Our school has a late math, early math setup. Half of the class starts school at eight and the other half starts at nine. They started doing it that way when we became overcrowded. All of us have late math, which means that technically Angela and Faye and I should start school with the twins at nine, but because of GATE, we start at eight.

Jury immediately started telling us about the pom-pom tackle game he and Judge had just finished. Pom-pom tackle is an outlawed game that most of the fifth-and sixth-grade boys play. It's kind of a combination of football, soccer, and field hockey and I don't know where it came from. When I started kindergarten the older boys were already playing it, but I've never seen it mentioned anywhere in any game book. Maybe I'll look it up one day on the Internet. I do know that there's a lot of rules, too many for any one kid to remember. It seems to me that all it takes to discover a new rule is for one kid to say it and a few others to claim they've heard it before.

The game consists of a pom-pom, which can be any object small enough to carry with one hand and large enough for everyone to see. Well, most everyone—last year we made a rule that kids can't play wearing their glasses. It's a very rough game. The main objective is to tackle the kid carrying the pom-pom before he scores or passes. That's why the game is outlawed at Faber. Most of the kids who have broken their glasses, arms, or legs during school, have broken them playing pom-pom tackle. Jury *lives* to play it. Normally, Angela and Faye wouldn't have any interest in hearing about a game, but Jury's story was pretty funny.

Apparently, Viet Nguyen, a fifth-grader, used some fancy footwork to tackle Percy Blake. "It was beautiful," Jury was saying. "Percy thought he was home free, probably gearing up for his victory dance"—at this point Jury stopped and did a few steps of Percy's imagined victory dance—"when Viet came out of nowhere, vaulted over Wayne's wheelchair, and tackled my boy Percy inches from the goal line."

"But not close enough to touch the line," Judge interrupted.

"Right, he couldn't touch the line." Jury took over again, but not before the brothers high-fived at exactly the same time. The girls and I started laughing again. Judge and Jury do that twin stuff all the time. As close as the rest of us are, we don't anticipate each other's actions the way the twins do. The high five also indicated that Judge and Jury were on the same team in this particular game, which isn't the way it usually goes. Both of them are such good players, the captains usually pick them first, forcing them to split up.

"Everything got quiet," Jury continued. "I don't know why, it was just one of those moments. I was on the ground with the rest of the guys, and I was thinking that Mr. C had probably busted us, but that wasn't it."

"What happened?" I asked.

"Everybody was looking at Percy, and Wayne was pointing at him." Jury stopped talking as he and Judge started cracking up.

"What?" Angela demanded. She's not known for her patience. Jury stopped laughing and looked directly at her. Faye and I moaned because we knew what was coming.

"Good things come to she who waits," Jury said.

Angela balled up her fist and shook it at Jury. "Well let's just wait and see what comes to you!" she said, but she was smiling. "Proceed please."

"Okay, so like I was saying, it was real quiet. Then we all heard this big ripping sound."

"Viet ripped his pants?" Faye asked.

Jury started laughing again, but he shook his head. "Not just his pants..."

"And not Viet—it was Percy," Judge added between laughs.

"It would have been funny enough without those checkerboard boxers!"

"Percy ripped his *boxers*?" Faye and Angela asked in disbelief.

That was it. We could hardly get it together before we entered the classroom. We were still laughing about the story when Miss Hoffer greeted us, blessed us, and started taking attendance. Miss Hoffer always says, "May God bless you with a wonderful day," or something similar. I know she's not supposed to pray like that in a public school, but who among us would tell? She's a good teacher.

When she called Percy's name, more than half of the class started laughing. News traveled fast.

Miss Hoffer stopped and looked up. "Where's Percy?" she asked.

Her question was answered with more laughter. It's not that we wanted to keep the story from her or anything like that. Everybody in the school knows that Miss Hoffer is the best teacher ever. Nobody volunteered because the kids who knew the story were busy whispering it to somebody who didn't or laughing too hard to talk.

"Jury, why don't you enlighten me? I enjoy a good laugh too."

I think Miss Hoffer has a special place in her heart for

Jury. Angela told me that she was in a student council meeting last year and she heard Miss Hoffer, next door in the teacher's lounge, defending Jury to Mr. Fritch, the physical education teacher. She didn't hear what Fritch said about Jury, but she heard Miss Hoffer call him "ridiculous." That's what made Angela stop to listen. She recognized Miss Hoffer's voice saying, "John Fritch, that's ridiculous. That child will make us all proud one day. I wonder if you wouldn't be just a bit more appreciative of Jury's wit if he was another student. Let's say a John Ross or Pat Bailey?"

Angela said Miss Hoffer sounded angry. We've never heard her raise her voice. We didn't discuss why Miss Hoffer said a John Ross or Pat Bailey. I think we both knew.

"Well, Miss Hoffer," Jury started, grinning all over himself. "You know how they say bad news will beat you home?" She didn't answer him. She squeezed her face up causing her eyebrows to almost meet. She was walking toward him. "Let's just call 6B our home away from home," he added.

That was it—the class just lost it. Miss Hoffer was standing next to Jury's desk. They started talking in low tones so I wasn't able to hear. Miss Hoffer came back near the front where she usually stands to take roll. She had a slight grin and I noticed the rim of her ears were red, but she didn't say anything. She continued to take roll.

I didn't get a chance to tell the Posse what was on my mind until lunch.

CHAPTER FIVE

The lunchroom is a joke. Every other period of the day, it's the multipurpose room. At lunchtime it's the multipurpose room with tables instead of the auditorium-style chairs. Our food is prepackaged, processed cardboard, complete with a drink and utensils that usually consist of a plastic spork. Next year in junior high school, we'll get real food but limited selections, and in high school, we'll get real food and multiple selections. This information is vital—I've done research. Looking at me, most people wouldn't guess, but food is important to me—to my whole family. As a family our best times have been spent around the dinner table.

Since I usually bring my lunch, my biggest problem with our lunchroom is the noise; I guess it's because the room was designed for lectures. It seems like every spoken word is magnified and held in some giant noise bubble just above our heads. The sixth-graders are a little better off than the other grades. We've claimed a section of tables behind some room dividers as our own. This section wasn't designated for us or anything like that. It just happens to be behind the area where the janitors store the dividers. There's only four tables back there, which means that about forty of us don't have to see the rest of the noisemakers.

We were all sitting at "our" table. As usual, the twins were arguing about their lunch money. Their mother gives one of them the money every morning; there doesn't seem to be a pattern as to which one gets it on a particular day. Without fail, the one who didn't get the money will argue that his brother didn't give him his fair share. This argument always takes place at the table *after* they both have their food. That's what makes it so silly and such a big waste of time.

"Okay, guys, I've got a mission for the Posse," I said, interrupting Judge, who had stood up to pull out his pants pockets. Judge sat down confident that he'd proven his pockets were empty.

"What kind of mission?" Angela asked as she peeled a boiled egg.

"Do you have to eat that thing around us?" Jury asked. Like the rest of us, he knew the whole area would soon stink like boiled egg.

Angela kept peeling. "No, you can leave."

"As I was saying, I've got a mission." I told them about the incident with Latecia. When I finished they were all staring at me, like they didn't understand or maybe they thought what I'd said was stupid. And then they all started talking at the same time.

"That's really scary," Faye said.

"I didn't know that little girl was deaf, did you?" Jury asked Judge. Judge nodded.

"We absolutely need to do something," Angela said. Jury says that Angela has a "righteous approach to life." I'm not sure if I know what he means by righteous—sometimes he says it like he respects her and other times he says it like it's an insult. But I do know we all think of her as going full speed ahead (again, Jury's words).

"Yes, but who will bell the cat?" Jury asked.

Again there was silence at the table. Angela looked like she was trying to contain her irritation. Judge just looked confused.

"Are we sure it's a bell we need?" Faye asked, sounding like a teacher.

"If what he means is some kind of warning, there's a yellow sign up by the light on Morgan that reads 'Deaf Child in Neighborhood,'" I said.

"Yeah, and another one near the highway," Judge said.

"So if signs don't work, what will?" Faye asked.

I knew I was running out of time. Some of the sixth-grade boys were throwing away their trays and sporks. One boy gave Jury a hard pat on the back as he passed, a signal that the after-lunch game of pom-pom tackle was only minutes away. I looked around the room for Mr. C—that's Mr. Carlisle, our vice-principal. His mission in life seems to be breaking up pom-pom tackle games.

Mr. C was standing by the dividers with his eyes and eyebrow (he has a single thick long eyebrow across his forehead) firmly focused on our table. Everybody knows Jury is the pom-pom tackle king of Faber.

"What's the plan?" Jury asked. He was getting antsy, looking around the room trying to determine today's pom-pom tackle strategy.

"I think we need to approach this logically," Angela said. She was crunching on a rice cake, of all things. The thought crossed my mind that Angela could be on some kind of diet. If she is, it makes about as much sense as me trying to grow dreadlocks. She's tall, a little taller than me, and she's not skinny like most of the girls our age. All the guys comment on her great shape. "First we need to figure out what the problem is," she continued.

"The problem is, drivers go down Tommy's street like those cartoon speed-racers, Angela."

"So the problem is the speed, Ju-ry?" Angela was playing some kind of logic game with us, but it wasn't working. We all just looked at her. Actually, Jury did mouth the word *Duh,* but he knew better than to say it out loud.

"The problem could be the amount of traffic, or the fact

that the little kids are playing in the street, or that there aren't enough police patrols or—"

"Okay, I see what you're saying," Faye interrupted.

I thought about it for a moment. "No, Angela, I think Jury's right—it's the speed. I doubt if there's anything we can do to reroute the traffic. It's the best route from downtown and the college to the highway."

"So the question is, what stops speeding cars?"

"Speed bumps," Jury answered. He could have been trying to be funny; he was definitely distracted with the next pom-pom tackle game. Faye's and Angela's faces lit up.

"That's it!" Faye said.

"What's it?"

"What you just said. We'll build a speed bump."

"We can't do that." Judge, the voice of reason, spoke.

"And why not?"

"Because." Judge looked at me to help him out, but the idea didn't sound that crazy to me. He looked at Jury, but Jury was wolfing down the last of his chocolate chip cookie and eyeing Mr. C.

"Because we're not street engineers, we're a group of sixth-graders. I figured we'd stand out there after school for a few days with signs or something. There's gotta be a law against homemade speed bumps," Judge said.

"There's a law against running over little deaf girls too, but that hasn't stopped the speeders!" Angela crossed her arms as if to say, "The righteous one has spoken."

"How hard could it be?" Faye asked.

We all looked at each other. Faye was right. How hard could it be to mix up some cement and pour it in the middle of the street?

"I wonder what's involved?" Judge asked. He was looking at Angela and rightfully so. She does seem to be a storehouse of unusual information.

"I remember watching my daddy and some other guys pouring our patio. I was pretty young when they did it, but I remember them putting down some wood so they'd know where to pour the cement..."

"Some guides," Judge interrupted.

"That makes sense," I added.

Jury was stacking up his stuff and looking around to see who else was ready for the game.

"But it seems like I remember them having a truck, you know the kind that has that rotating vat on it?"

"But we wouldn't need that much cement," I told Angela.

"That's true."

"Right, we could use a plastic garbage can to mix it," Faye said.

Jury stood up. "Okay, guys, this is the plan. Judge, you and Tommy tell the guys that we're playing on the west field. I'll go out to the east field and Mr. C will follow me. I'll shoot a few baskets with the little kids. I'll stay out there long enough for him to think we're not playing today. He'll leave, and then I'll meet you on the west field."

31

"Jury, we were discussing *Tommy's* situation here," Angela said, sounding like somebody's mother.

"Oh yeah. Tommy, Judge and I will spend the night this weekend. Angela and Faye will get the prices for the cement and find us a couple of boards to use as guides. We'll mix the cement and hide it in your garage. After everybody goes to sleep in your house, we'll get up and make the speed bump. It'll have the rest of the night to dry." He left the table without looking back at us.

The three of us sat there grinning. "Well, I guess this meeting of the Plank Posse is adjourned," Judge finally announced.

I thought about the speed bump for the rest of the day. I didn't get a chance to talk to the Posse again after lunch because Jury's game plan worked. Mr. C followed him to the east field while the rest of us were on the west field dividing into teams. Wayne volunteered his hat for us to use as the pom-pom, provided we were careful not to tear it. We all agreed, but unfortunately it didn't survive the game. Also unfortunately, we later learned it was his brother's hat.

CHAPTER SIX

By the end of the school day, Angela had written a list of things to do to accomplish our plan. There were about fifteen items, things like checking the price of cement, buying a garbage can, and so on. Most of the items had Angela's or Faye's names next to them. The two things I had to do were simple: find out if Judge and Jury could spend Saturday night at my house and determine what time my family goes to sleep. Actually, the list said, "Study target family's nightly ritual," but I figured that that was just Angela being dramatic.

I can do this, I told myself. *We* can do this. Faye had drawn a sketch, a sort of blueprint, of the bump on the back of Angela's list. It was real, the drawing made it real for me. We were actually going to make a speed bump in the middle of my street! When you look up *friends* in the dictionary, there ought to be a picture of the Posse.

Faye had to stay after school for some kind of meeting so she didn't walk home with us. Jury always teases Faye and

Angela about all their meetings—he says they would go to a meeting to plan the next meeting.

"When you get home, Tommy, you should watch the traffic for a while so we can figure out the best place to put the bump."

"What do you mean, Angela?" While tripping on what great friends they are, I figured I had missed something. "Won't we put it right in the middle?"

"I doubt it. By the time the drivers get to the middle of the block, they're already at full speed. You want to slow them down before then."

She was right. I hadn't thought about that.

"Yeah, and if we put it in the wrong place, we could cause somebody to mess up their car." Judge stopped walking and started laughing. Jury seemed to know what was on his mind and started cracking up too. "Jury, remember that time—"

Jury started nodding before Judge could finish. "I remember. Grandpa was so mad . . ." He couldn't finish, either, he was laughing so hard.

Angela and I just looked at them. It must be nice to share so much common experience with someone.

"What?" Angela finally demanded.

"Grandpa used to take us for rides when we were little. Usually, just before bringing us home, he would take us over to the campus."

Jury took over. "You know how when you go down certain hills you get that tickle in your belly?"

Angela and I nodded.

"We liked to go down that hill behind the Pugh Business and Industry building. I think Grandpa liked to do it too, but he would always wait for us to ask. 'Take us down the hill, Grandpa. Take us down the hill!'" Jury said this last part in a little kid's voice that made me and Angela start to laugh too.

"He had a new Buick LeSabre," Judge piped in.

"Yeah, that green one. It was a Sunday afternoon during the summer so there weren't many students around. Grandpa drove through the campus, building up his speed. By the time we got to the hill, he was probably going about forty miles an hour. It was going to be a good one. We got to the hill and started down."

"All three of us yelled *wheeee!*"

"Until we hit it—boom!" At this point Jury doubled over with laughter. Judge finished.

"They'd put up a speed bump since the last time we'd driven there," Judge explained. "When we went over the bump, it sounded and felt like the whole car was falling apart."

"You know how my grandfather is, he thinks *darn* is a swear word?" Jury said.

We nodded. Both sets of their grandparents are very religious.

"He got out of the car using words we'd never heard before. He wanted to be angry at somebody, probably us, but we were just two little guys in kindergarten. And to make matters worse..." Judge glanced at Jury. I think he was trying to decide if he should tell the rest, but Jury was too busy laughing to notice. "Jury started repeating one of the swear words Grandpa had said. Even with the car making all kinds of strange noises, he took us to see a movie so Jury would forget the word before we got home."

"Is that why we went to the movies that day? I never knew that."

"Yes, you did. Grandma still talks about it. Grandpa doesn't believe in going to see movies on Sundays."

Jury nodded in agreement.

Judge continued. "As soon as we got home, we started telling our parents and our grandma about what happened. We told them all about the movie and the junk we'd eaten. Grandpa probably thought he was safe. Then Jury said"— and here Judge used *his* little kid's voice—"and the best part was when we went down the hill where somebody had put in a blanking speed bump."

"Only I said the real word," Jury explained, as if we didn't know.

We all laughed again, and then talked some more about our own speed bump. The twins assured me that they didn't expect a problem getting permission to spend the night. By the time we got to my turnoff, I was in a great mood. But when I reached the spot where I heard Quinn cry out the day before, everything became serious again.

CHAPTER SEVEN

As I got closer to home, I saw that the bottom half of my street was jam-packed with people and vans. "Oh no," I said as I took off running down the hill. I was sure one of the kids had gotten hit by a car. I'm ashamed to say it now, but I prayed that it was anyone but Quinn. As I got closer, I could see that the vehicle that I thought was an ambulance was actually an Action Team news van. I quickly scanned the crowd. I never realized before how many little kids there are in the neighborhood.

Last month our cousin Mimi sent Quinn a thingamajig for her ponytails. It's one of those real simple million-dollar ideas. With a few twists and turns, Quinn can make all kinds of different hairstyles that start from a ponytail. That's how I spotted Quinn in the crowd—by her hair. She was wearing some kind of strange triple-twisted topknot. I ran to her and snatched her up into my arms.

"Tommy, put me down!" she squealed. She had the nerve to sound embarrassed. This from the mushiest kid in the world. All her little friends started laughing.

"What's going on?" I asked.

"Somebody put some letters on our window."

"What?" I asked, but I didn't wait for her answer. I turned to face our house. From what Quinn had said, I expected to see some envelopes containing letters taped to our window. What I saw instead were three large red Ks. A chill ran down my back. KKK on my window? It just didn't compute. I moved through the crowd, closer to the house, stopping less than four feet from the large picture window. I stared at each letter. I tried to picture the hand that had held the can of spray paint—impossible. That hand didn't belong in Plank, not in my hometown.

"Step back, kid, you're creating a shadow."

I looked around at the man who was, apparently, speaking to me. He touched me on the shoulder and, even though I watched him doing it, I jumped.

"Relax, kid. I'm just trying to take a picture here."

I noticed the camera he was holding. "Why?" I asked.

"This is front-page news." He stepped in front of me, forcing me back a few feet, and took his picture. "The problem is, as usual, they're going to get it out before us." The camera guy nodded his head.

I looked in the direction of his nod. He was talking

about a woman who was holding a big, heavy-looking video camera on her shoulder, and another woman holding a microphone.

I repeated the camera guy's words to myself. Okay, my house is violated, and he's complaining about television news being faster than the morning newspaper. As soon as I heard the words in my mind I realized how little I cared about his issues and how I was wasting time.

When I moved closer to the woman with the microphone, I saw it was Mariama Scott. "Too bad the twins aren't here," I thought. Mariama Scott must be one of the prettiest news-people in the country. She's made Judge and Jury—okay, me too—fans of the six o'clock news.

Even with Mariama Scott so close, my heartbeat had returned to normal. My sister and her friends were safe. Some idiot had written on our windows, but letters can't hurt anybody. I studied the pretty reporter. She looked even better in real life. Her slim brown hand held the micro-phone, her left hand. I noticed because she was wearing a ring that caught the sun at an angle that sent a sparkling flash across the crowd.

An engagement ring. Angela would be proud of me; I don't usually notice those kinds of things. Some lucky guy was going to marry Foxy Four (that's what we call her, because she's on Channel Four). I made a mental note to tell the guys.

I watched her mike hand as it stretched out and stopped just short of my mother's mouth. *My mother's mouth!* The words screamed in my head as I nudged past an old woman and pushed my way into the crowd. Stopping directly in front of my mother, I shook my head hard enough to almost send my glasses sailing through the air. My mother frowned like she understood, but then broke into a big grin.

"This is my son, Tom."

I couldn't believe my ears. Did she think I was trying to get her to introduce me? Foxy Four was saying something into the mike. I tried to think like Angela. She always knows what to do, what to say to adults. Foxy Four was smiling at me.

"What's your reaction to the vandalism, Tommy?"

The microphone was now almost touching my mouth.

"We don't wish to make a statement at this time," I mumbled as I turned away from the camera.

For a split second, she was at a loss for words. But Foxy Four quickly recovered and moved the mike back toward my mother. I felt a hand squeezing my arm. I turned, expecting to see Quinn, but was shocked to find my father.

"Are you all right, son?"

"Dad, you've got to stop her. She doesn't know what she's doing."

He looked across the street at Quinn and her friends.

"What's she doing?"

"Not Quinn, Mom! Stop her before she gets us all killed!" My father is a man of few words. He didn't have to tell me to go inside; I knew when I saw his right eyebrow shoot up that I had behaved badly. With my father you can get away with just about anything as long as you don't "behave badly" while you're doing it. It was a lesson well learned during his childhood.

Unlike my mother's parents, my father's parents weren't sent to the internment camps during World War II. My grandmother was still in Japan, but my grandfather's family lived in this country. They had already moved "inland," as they call it—from California to Kentucky. I think that, deep down, my grandfather believes that what saved his family the financial and mental humiliation of the camps was their "stellar behavior." This conversation always upsets my mother and, actually, my father too. My parents believe that Grandfather's family was so poor and in such a poor community, they were never considered a security threat. My mother says that if Grandfather's family had owned the same kind of rich farmland her family in California owned, they would have been interned too. It was during the internment that her family's land was stolen from them. My dad seems to believe this too, but he was raised not to make waves and it's a hard habit to break. The only time he really lets loose is when he's playing his video games. The man is a PlayStation maniac.

"Tommy, do you want to explain what you were talking about out there?" he asked when he joined me later in the kitchen.

It was a trick question. What he was really saying was I *better* tell him what I was talking about. "Dad, Mom's going to get herself killed. She can't stand out there talking to Foxy—I mean, Mariama Scott—about those letters. She should have washed them off as soon as she saw them."

He sat down next to me. "Do you know the difference between publicity and advertising?"

This was a surprise—I was expecting a reprimand. "No," I said, having no clue about what he was trying to say.

"You pay to advertise. What your mother got today was publicity for the rally. Those jerks did us a favor."

I wanted to slap myself on the side of the head like a cartoon character, but I was pretty sure that would've been behaving badly. "Dad, do you know who the Ku Klux Klan are?"

"Of course I do."

"You haven't studied about hate crimes, but I have," I said.

He took off his glasses and wiped his eyes. He gave me the patient but annoyed look he used to give Quinn when she'd asked one question too many. "Son, I didn't have to study hate crimes. I've lived them."

His statement silenced me.

"I can understand your being afraid—"

"I'm not afraid!" I cried.

"All right, son. I *am* afraid for her. But I know that the more attention focused on her, the safer she is."

I thought about that. He had a point. Okay, I decided, publicity can be good.

CHAPTER EIGHT

The carnival atmosphere in front of my house lasted for about another hour and a half. My dad eventually went back outside, but even the thought of Foxy Four couldn't get me to return. At one point I looked out and saw Judge and Jury, but it was at least another half hour before they came to the door.

"Why aren't you out front?" Judge asked.

"Did you see her?" Jury asked, before I could answer his brother. I turned from them and started walking toward the stairs; they followed, going on and on about Foxy Four.

"She smiled at me," Jury said more than once when we were in my bedroom.

"What's wrong with you?" Judge finally asked when I hadn't said anything for a while.

I was sitting on the bed. Jury was still standing and Judge was sitting at my desk. Jury had a goofy grin on his face, no doubt visions of him and Foxy Four dancing in his head.

"What's wrong?" Judge asked again. Most people think of the twins as kind of like a single unit, two halves of a whole, but they're so different. If I had to choose, I think I'd pick Judge as my favorite of the two, but I doubt if either of them would guess that. The difference is in fractions, but Judge is the better friend. He really cares about people. Jury does too, but he can be a little self-absorbed.

"I'm really worried about this rally."

"I know."

"You do?"

"Yeah, you're afraid your mother could get hurt—"

"Or do something to embarrass all of us," Jury interrupted.

"You guys have read about this stuff," I said. "We can't mess around with the Klan."

"Tommy, she wasn't messing around with them. She was doing her thing and they're messing with her."

"Judge is right, man. Sometimes you've got to take a stand. Speaking of which, we got the go-ahead to stay over Saturday night."

It took me a moment to figure out what he was saying.

"Angela called. In fact, she's the one who told us what was happening over here. She saw it on a news break. She's got some news of her own, but she didn't trust me with it. She said she would call you."

"Bad news?" I asked Jury, but they both shrugged. By the time my mother and sister came in and my father had beaten the twins at his newest favorite video game, Angela still hadn't called. My father and I dropped Judge and Jury off when we went out to pick up pizzas for dinner. We were having pizza a lot lately it seemed.

When we returned, my mother was sitting in her grandmother's rocker, holding the abacus. My mother sits in the old rocker or she holds the abacus when she's not a happy camper. For her to be doing both was not a good sign at all. As I set the paper plates and napkins on the table, I could heard the chair squeaking as the wooden abacus balls clicked against each other. I know she knows how to count on it. When her mother was interned she learned math both ways, American and Japanese. A lot of internees won't talk about the experience, but my grandmother wasn't one of them. She died when I was little and I don't remember her. My mother says she died of a broken heart—her country betrayed her.

I went upstairs and told Quinn to wash her hands for dinner. My father was in the family room, pretending like he was reading something important. I could see it was a video magazine.

"Should I ask Mom to come to dinner?"

"Where is she?"

"In the dining room."

"In the chair?"

"Yes. She has the abacus too."

He looked up from his magazine. "Is the light on?"

"No."

He thought about it. "Ask her if you can make her some tea." He smiled. His idea pleased him. He looked back down at his magazine. I assumed he wasn't all that hungry either.

The chair was no longer moving. Her eyes were closed. I couldn't see them in the darkened room, but I knew they were closed.

"Mom, would you like a cup of tea? I can make a pot and leave it here."

"That would be nice, Tommy."

I didn't walk away. I could tell she wanted to say something else to me.

"Tommy, have you seen pictures of me when I was a little girl?"

"Yes."

"I was a happy little girl. I giggled all the time, even more than Quinn. I had a doll, an Oban dancer doll. She was my prized possession, but I can't remember her name."

"Oh." I didn't know what to say.

"I was a happy little girl, but I don't know if my mother was ever happy."

"Why not?"

"My mother lived in the camp from 1942 to 1945. Her parents wouldn't allow any pictures to be taken of them in there. My uncle was born in 1945 and there are lots of his baby pictures. And there's a few of her older brother and sister before the camp, but none of my mother. Life was so difficult after the camps, years went by before pictures became important again. The only pictures we have of her are at age seven and on her wedding day. I don't know if she was happy."

"I'm sure she was happy sometimes."

"I didn't see it. She smiled sometimes, but I don't remember the sound of her laughter. Tommy, I think that what I'm doing now would have made her happy. I believe she's smiling right now."

I could hear the tears in her voice. "I'm sure she is, Mom."

Later, as I sat eating pizza with Quinn, but not quite enjoying it, I had to wonder, am *I* proud of *my* mother?

CHAPTER NINE

My mother was still sitting in the rocker by the time Quinn and I had finished dinner. If parents knew how much we worry about them, they'd be more careful about what they let us see.

After dinner, I cleaned the kitchen. Quinn sensed the mood in the house and stayed close to me.

"Do you want me to help?" she asked while I was stacking the dishwasher.

"Sure, why don't you sweep?" I got the broom from the side of the refrigerator and handed it to her. "Have you finished your homework?"

Normally, she would have rolled her eyes at me for asking such a question, but she smiled. I was trying to keep things normal and she appreciated that.

"I still have to read my social studies."

I debated if I should turn on the dishwasher. It's loud, and my mother was just a few feet away.

"Tommy, is Mommy in trouble?" She was watching the trash slide off the dustpan into the garbage can. She was holding it up too high, running the risk of letting some of the trash fall back to the floor, but I didn't say anything.

"No, Mommy's not in trouble. Not at all. You shouldn't worry about her."

She moved closer to me and whispered, "Why is she in the rocker?"

"She has a lot of stuff to think about. We have to be patient and not add to her..." I hesitated, wanting to use the right word. "Her concerns."

Quinn nodded like we were sharing a big secret. She's a great kid. She put the broom and dustpan away. "I'm going to heat up Mommy's tea," she announced, as she started out in the direction of the dining room.

I decided not to turn on the dishwasher. The thought occurred to me to stay with Quinn, but I figured I was taking my big brother role a little too seriously. She can handle the microwave without my input.

The telephone was ringing just as I started to enter my bedroom. It was in the hallway between my room and Quinn's. "Hello?" I answered.

"Hey, Tommy. Has all the excitement died down over there?"

"I guess so. Jury said you have some news?"

"Is this a good time?" Angela asked.

"Hold on." I dragged the cord into my room and closed the door. "Okay, it's good."

"We've got a problem."

"What?"

"We've been talking about concrete, but street bumps are made out of—"

"Asphalt," I said with her. I hadn't thought about it until that moment.

"Right. I talked to one guy at the hardware store on the phone."

"You had him reading packages to you?"

"Sure, why not?"

"Did he know you're a kid?"

Angela didn't answer me right away. I wondered if she was taking issue with me calling her a kid. I think she forgets sometimes.

"He knew I was a potential customer. I didn't feel the need to state my age. Anyway, Tommy, I guess there's a reason they put those sawhorses up when they fix potholes in the street. The shortest curing time was seventy-two hours."

"Seventy-two hours!"

"That's right. But that's okay. The way I figure it, we can put up a barrier too. The only time there's any traffic around here is on weekdays. It can dry all day Sunday."

"Angela, there's no way the neighbors are going to leave it alone." At that moment Quinn stuck her head in my door.

She was dressed for bed. "I'm going to sleep, Tommy," she said. I think she wanted to kiss me good night since, apparently, our parents were taking the night off. I wasn't ready to take my substitute parent role that far. I told Angela to hold on a minute, then I told Quinn I'd check on her when I finished with my call. That seemed to be enough for her; she nodded and left.

"Why not? Isn't it to their advantage to have the bump too?" Angela asked, not commenting on what I'd said to Quinn.

I started making noises about dropping the whole idea.

"No, we can still do this," she said firmly, righteously. "If it was important this morning, it's important now. I've got a book here—a do-it-yourself home repair book. It shows how to make a concrete walkway. I figured Faye and I can make the form boards—"

"What's that?"

"The boards that will hold up the sides of the bump while you guys are pouring it. It'll just be some connected two-by-fours. Okay, this page I'm looking at right now is for concrete steps, but I'm sure we can improvise."

"Angela—"

"Tommy, don't flake out on us. It's a good idea. Sometimes you have to stand up for your good ideas."

I remembered hearing similar words earlier. "Angela—" I started again, but again she interrupted.

"Go tuck Quinn in. Sleep on it. We'll talk tomorrow."

I started to argue that I wasn't going to "tuck Quinn in," but I replayed her tone in my head and realized that Angela wasn't teasing me. "Yeah, I better go see about her. My parents are really out of it."

"I guess," she agreed. "I would be too."

Quinn wouldn't let me leave her bedroom until she told me her latest jokes. Usually her jokes are pretty lame, and these were no exception, but we both laughed for at least twenty minutes.

"Okay, I'm turning out the light," I told her as I stood by the door with my hand on the switch.

"One more, Tommy."

"Okay, what?"

"Where does the general put his army?"

"I don't know, where?"

"In his sleevy."

"Say good night, Quinn."

"Good night, Quinn."

When I came out, my mother was standing by Quinn's door. She didn't say anything. She was just standing there. She looked tiny to me. She is small, about five two, but she looked smaller than usual. For a second it felt like I was the parent and she was the child.

It frightened me.

She hugged me tightly, like she was afraid to let go. When she did let go, I said, "Good night, Mom." She touched my cheek and smiled.

That night I didn't hear my parents talking.

CHAPTER TEN

At school on Thursday, everybody was talking about what had happened at my house. By second period I was tired of the sound of my own voice. "No, I don't know who put the letters on our windows. No, I don't think the police have arrested anybody. No, I don't know anything about Mariama Scott!"

Unlike our GATE teacher, Miss Hoffer didn't question me as soon as I walked into our regular classroom. As she was walking around the room, taking attendance and telling us what to expect for the day, she simply paused by my desk and let her hand rest on my shoulder. I don't know why, but the weight of her hand seemed to trigger tears that I had to fight hard to hold back.

By first recess, I was determined to surround myself with the Posse and talk about the speed bump and only the speed bump. I pulled Faye aside just before we went out.

"Faye, all this talk about the Klan and stuff is really messing with my head. Will you run interference, if you can?"

I knew what I was doing. Faye is the mothering one in our group. She nodded and jumped in front of me like she was a three-hundred-pound bodyguard. Since nobody was trying to rush me, the only person she slowed down was me. But as soon as we got outside, she told a group of fifth-grade girls who were approaching me, "Tommy doesn't want to talk about it." Then she waved them away with her hand, adding, "Give him a little space."

The fifth-graders looked at each other and then at Faye as if they thought she was tripping, which she was, but they left me alone so I was grateful.

"Thanks, Faye."

"No problem." She looked around like one of those secret service guys you see in movies. All she needed was an earphone held in place with constant pressure from her index finger, and a pair of those dark sunglasses, and she would have been set. When some boys looked like they wanted to say something to me, she shook her head and waved them away.

It cracked me up. I couldn't wait to tell the twins about how goofy she was acting.

The other members of the Posse were waiting for us in the usual place. Jury was already looking around, itching to get a pom-pom tackle game going. Angela was obviously fed up with his mania.

"What took you so long?" Judge asked.

"I had to protect Tommy from the masses," Faye volunteered, still standing in front of me.

Judge looked to me for an answer, but I only smiled and shook my head. I was afraid I would start laughing if I had to explain. That wouldn't have been right considering Faye was only doing what I had asked.

Angela brought everybody up on what we'd talked about the night before. "I know my father has some two-by-fours in his toolshed. Faye, if you can come over right after school, we can put the form board together. Can you guys go to the hardware store?"

"Yeah, but it's not like we'll be driving. How are we supposed to get the bag of cement or mortar or whatever we're using to Tommy's?" Judge asked.

We all looked at Jury. Angela is the Plan Master, true enough, but Jury's good with missions that require a degree of deviance. "Why are you all looking at me? What am I, the local car thief or something?"

We all laughed. "Okay, seriously, why don't we just take our old wagon," he said, and looked at Judge for support. "We'll go to the store, put the bag in the wagon, and roll it over to Tommy's." Then Jury looked at me. "How likely is it that your parents will be home?"

"Today?" I asked.

Jury nodded.

"My father won't be home. But with this rally stuff, my

mother's schedule hasn't been too predictable. But I don't see why she would pay any attention to a wagon, especially if we cover the cargo with our book bags and jackets."

"What about Quinn?" Faye asked.

"Quinn won't be a problem. She'll be playing with her friends. She won't pay any attention to us. How much is the mortar, Angela?"

"We should be able to get all we'll need for less than ten dollars."

I pulled the twenty dollars I had been saving for a Father's Day gift from my pocket. "This should cover it," I said as I handed it to Jury. As luck would have it, Mr. C rounded the corner just in time to see the money change hands.

He was, no doubt, tracking Jury to determine if a pom-pom tackle game was in the making. Seeing the money pass hands brought him to a complete stop. He looked at Jury and then me. He waited, like he expected us to explain what was going on.

"Hi, Mr. C," Angela said. When he heard her voice, he dropped the attitude. Everybody knows that Angela is one of his favorite students.

"Angela," was all he said with a smile and a slight nod of his head.

Jury made a production of taking out his wallet and putting the twenty in it. He smiled at Mr. C when he finished. "Looks like an early spring, wouldn't you say, Mr. C?"

He was pushing it. I know Mr. C isn't one of his favorite people, but sometimes Jury doesn't know when to stop. Thankfully, Mr. C mumbled something about Groundhog Day and continued along his way.

"You really ought to give him a break, Jury Jenkins. He's not the enemy."

When Angela uses Jury's whole name, you know she's angry.

Jury placed his hand over his heart. "The enemy of pom-pom tackle is thy enemy as well."

Faye walked over and stood between Angela and Jury. "Come on, guys. Recess is almost over and I need to go to the restroom."

Jury pointed in the direction of the girls' bathroom.

"I know where it is, Ju-ry! I was waiting to see if there's anything else we need to know about the bump."

They all looked at me. I knew it was probably my last chance to call the whole thing off. I had my doubts about the plan, but somebody had to do something for the little kids that played on my street. Somehow that somebody had become me. "I think we're all set," I said.

CHAPTER ELEVEN

I was ambushed. After recess, without Faye to protect me, I was hit when and where I least expected it. One of my most favorite people in the world had lulled me into a false sense of security and, as Jury would say, pulled the rug out from under me.

"Okay, class, before we write in our journals, I want to spend a little time talking about another matter," Miss Hoffer began.

I felt the blood rushing to my face even before she had announced the subject—I just knew what it would be.

She started off telling the class something my mother has said many times. "During World War II, only ten people were convicted of spying for Japan. All of them were Caucasian. Nevertheless, the U.S. government moved many Japanese Americans into internment camps in the belief that they would attempt to aid the enemy."

I studied the class for a reaction, but there wasn't one. I couldn't tell if they didn't understand what she was saying or if they didn't care.

Then she told us pretty much the same story my mother had told me and Quinn about Vincent Chin. That's when they started to pay attention, maybe because it was a modern-day story about a guy not much older than us. Next she went into a brief history of Asians in America. She talked about something I had never heard of, the Webb Act. Apparently, by the early 1890s, Japanese immigrants in California were doing so well as farmers that white Californians were starting to feel threatened. In 1905 some farmers in San Francisco got together and had a meeting. By 1913 California had passed a law to keep Japanese from buying land.

One time I'd asked my father what brought his family from the West Coast to Kentucky, and he didn't know; I bet it had something to do with that law. His family was very isolated from the bulk of the Japanese Americans who lived on the West and East Coasts.

Miss Hoffer wrote the word *Nisei* on the board and explained that it meant the child of Japanese immigrants. I took notes, like I always do, but I could feel the staring eyes of my classmates. I'd never felt so self-conscious in my life. I wondered how Judge, Jury, and Angela had managed to sit through so many lessons about slavery and the

Underground Railroad without wanting to dig a hole to crawl into.

A few of the kids groaned when she mentioned various injustices, but most of them sat quietly and listened.

"I know a woman who was interned when she was a child," Miss Hoffer continued. "She's spoken to my classes in the past. She's agreed to come in next week to tell you students and the other sixth-grade class about it. Some of you might know her. She used to sub here around the time you would have been first or second-graders. Her name is Mrs. Hayakawa."

Again, hearing the Japanese name, my classmates all seemed to shift in their chairs and look at me. What was I supposed to do? Stand up and make an announcement? "No, I don't know the woman, but I'm sure she's a fine human being!"

"I remember Mrs. Hayakawa!" somebody said from the other side of the room, and thankfully the attention was finally diverted off me. Miss Hoffer went on with her lesson. At the end, she came back to the Vincent Chin rally, telling the class that she would give extra credit to anybody who participated. Yup, I said to myself, it all starts and ends with that darn rally.

I seriously considered not going to lunch.

A less hungrier guy would have spent his lunch hour in the library or volunteering in the office. Luckily, my friends didn't talk about Miss Hoffer's lesson during lunch. At first I thought they were trying to spare me, but the fact is, we rarely talk about schoolwork.

"How about a game of basketball after lunch?" Jury asked.

Everybody looked up from what they were doing.

"What?" I asked.

"He's wearing me down, guys. I'm beginning to think it's just not worth it anymore."

"What?" Angela asked.

"I don't know why Mr. C hates seeing us having fun, but he does. I'm just getting tired of the hassle."

"Who are you?" Judge asked. "What have you done with my brother?"

"Aren't you sick of it?" He looked at Judge and then me.

"It's just what I have to do to play. You want to play basketball, you find a round ball and a net. If you want to play pom-pom tackle, you hide from Mr. C," Judge said.

And well said it was. I nodded in agreement.

"Angela, Faye?" Jury asked.

That surprised me. He knows they couldn't care less about pom-pom tackle.

"You know how I feel about that stupid game, but it seems to make you happy. I say play your game and let the bones fall where they may." We all laughed. How odd for Angela to make a joke.

"You know, I think my parents are a couple of old

hippies," Faye said. She has a habit of changing the subject, but usually ties everything up in the end.

We all nodded. Faye's parents are a little older than the rest of our parents. I know that they're very fair-minded, liberal people, but I didn't know where she was going with this or why she had brought it up.

"They think that, as a group, our generation is really not taking advantage of our resources," Faye continued.

"What does that mean?" Jury asked.

"They say that we care about stuff, just as kids always have, but we don't make anybody listen to us. When my mother read that there's schools that don't let kids use their lockers, she lost it." Faye stopped and took a bite of her apple.

"What do you mean, won't let the kids use the lockers?" I asked.

Faye held up her finger until she was done chewing. "In some places, the administration has prohibited the use of lockers since some kids were storing drugs in them. So now, all the kids have to lug around their books in a book bag all day. The same article talked about how in other places, they've decided that drugs and weapons are transported in book bags so *they've* been banned. My mother was upset because in both cases we're talking about just a few kids spoiling it for the rest and getting away with it. The article said some kids lug around books that are half their body weight. It's causing back problems. My mother said that in her day, there would have been big protests." She took another bite. "I guess that's why she's so excited about your mother's rally."

"She is?" I asked. "She thinks this rally is a good thing?"

"Of course, don't you?"

All eyes were on me. How could I tell them that I thought the rally was the worst idea I'd heard in all my years? Why was this so easy for them? "How would you feel if it was *your* mother doing it?" I gave each of them a brief look in the eye.

Faye and Jury answered together. *"Proud."*

CHAPTER TWELVE

Luckily, I didn't have to explain how much I hated being on display. Jury saved me by changing the subject. He said, "I guess I owe it to the guys to play, don't I?" He was back on the pom-pom tackle subject.

I doubt if any of us saw his enthusiasm as anything so noble, but we nodded. He pushed his tray away and stood.

"So let the games continue," he said, and then left the table.

"And everybody calls *me* dramatic," Angela commented.

After lunch I played in one of the most energized pom-pom tackle games ever. Mr. C caught us and broke it up while we were tied, three to three. As we were lining up outside to go back to class, guys were still arguing about which team would've won. Just as I was getting comfortable with the idea that things were back to normal, Nancy Richards, a classmate who was standing behind me in line, tapped me on the shoulder.

"Tommy, that stuff Miss Hoffer was saying about your people today, it made me really sad. I'm so sorry for you."

I looked around to see if anybody heard her. Most of the class was listening to the pom-pom tackle argument. The ones that weren't didn't seem to be paying any attention to me. "Me and my people thank you, Nancy."

She smiled. My sarcasm was lost on her.

Once, this lady attempted to tell me about her son, who fought and died in Vietnam. I figured she must have thought I was Vietnamese or, being Asian, I reminded her of the war. The conversation made me very uncomfortable. There she was in the grocery store aisle, crying to me about a horrible war that divided the country, expecting me to say something comforting about it now, over thirty years later. But Nancy's comment was the first time anybody my age had ever said anything like that to me. And I had my own mother to thank for it.

I tried to spend the rest of the day with my head buried in my books. At one point Angela, who was passing out papers for the teacher, bent down and whispered in my ear, "Get over it, Tommy." When I looked up at her she gave me a look of disappointment that my own mother hasn't given me since I was potty training.

I wanted to jump up and explain to her that I couldn't get over it; I couldn't even define "it." I got my chance when we were walking home from school. Judge and Jury stayed on campus to try to finish the game Mr. C had broken up. After the game, they were going to go home to get the wagon. They tried to talk me into staying too, but I wasn't sure if my mother was going to be home for Quinn. I never did find out where Faye was. It was just me and Angela.

"It's easier for black people," I told her.

She started laughing. "Tommy, no matter what the topic, nothing is ever easier for black folks!"

"It has to be. You've got the numbers and the history. They think they know your story."

"That's why it's not easier. Everything they think they know is negative. At least nobody questions your intelligence, or your honesty."

"No, but has the office ever called you down to see if you can translate Vietnamese?"

Angela laughed again. "No, that hasn't happened, but I've been asked some pretty stupid questions."

"Like how to prepare sushi?"

"Try sweet potato pie, dirty rice, and chitlins."

"What's dirty rice?"

"I have no idea, but black people somewhere must eat it. The point is, that's what being a minority is. The majority expects you to speak for the group. You can't hide who you are, Tommy. Nobody is going to let you forget that you're different, so you might as well accept it and be proud of it!"

"Do I have to flaunt it?"

"It doesn't matter. To some people, your just being here is flaunting it."

"Don't you get tired of it?"

"Of course I do. But it's kind of cool too."

"How?"

"I don't know." She stopped walking, like she couldn't think about what she was trying to say with her feet still moving. "Maybe I'm wrong, but sometimes when I read the paper and I see how messed up the world is, I feel like there's still hope."

"How do you see hope in what you call messed up?" We started walking again.

"Because we haven't had our chance to run things yet. We've got to do better."

"We who?"

"Women, minorities, all the *wes*. Maybe when we get our chance, we'll make things right." She looked at me like she expected me to say something. I didn't. "It's what your mom is trying to do."

"Yeah, but why *my* mother?"

"Why do *we* have to be the ones to make the speed bump?"

This time I stopped walking. "That's not the same, Angela!"

"How is it different?"

Surprisingly, I didn't have a quick answer. I thought about it for a moment. "Somebody has to slow these people down before they kill one of the kids."

"And somebody needs to stop racists before they kill the next Vincent Chin."

Was she right? She's Angela, and Angela's usually right. I looked at her again, and she didn't gloat. I must admit though, she didn't look nearly as sure about herself as she usually does.

"I could be wrong, Tommy."

"You?"

She laughed. "Yeah, you're right. I'm not wrong."

My street was quiet. Quinn, Latecia, and two other little girls were playing in our yard.

Each of them said, "Hi, Tommy," and each waited for a personal hello.

The first thing I noticed when I got inside was how clean everything was. The house usually looks pretty good, but there's no mistaking people live in it. I could tell my mother had had one of her cleaning sprees. Sometimes, especially when she's got something on her mind, she cleans excessively. One time Jury was visiting while she was trying to clean around us. He said she reminded him of a humming-bird on caffeine. He finally said he had to go home because watching her was making him tired. Considering how things looked when I left for school, I was tired just thinking about how busy she must have been.

I got a stack of comic books and sat at the kitchen table.

I figured it was a good place to wait for the twins.

"Where's Mom?" I asked Quinn when she came in for a drink.

"It's not my day to watch her."

I looked up from the comic. Quinn was smiling. She knew she'd said something kind of cool and she was waiting for my reaction.

"Not your day, huh?" I balled up my comic and hit her on the head with it. She laughed and ran outside to tell her friends.

I must have gotten into my reading, because I was surprised when I heard the twins outside teasing the girls.

"That was quick," I told them as I watched Judge pull the wagon into the garage.

"Have wagon, will travel," Jury said.

"We weren't able to finish the game. Mr. C was everywhere," Judge explained.

"Did you have any trouble at the hardware store?" I asked.

"Nope."

I lifted the bag out. It was heavier than it looked. "Premium Dual-Purpose Thin-Set Mortar," I read.

"Hooked on phonics worked for you!" Jury teased.

I ignored him. "Fifty-pound bag. Do you think this will be enough?"

"It better be, that sucker was heavy!"

"Like you did your fair share of pulling," Judge said.

I interrupted before it could turn into a Judge and Jury moment. "It says thin-set. What we're planning to do is set it thick, isn't it?"

They gave me blank looks and we all started laughing.

"Like we know. Your guess is as good as ours," Jury said.

"The way I figure it, this is enough to make a bump in the road and a bump will slow them down. That's all we want, right?" Judge asked.

I nodded. "Things should be getting busy out there soon. Let's go watch the traffic so we can figure out where to put the bump." I hid the bag under a pile of old clothes. I figured that with all my mother had to do, looking under old clothes was the last thing on her mind.

We gathered up the comics and three cans of soda. We found a good spot on Latecia's lawn. Mrs. Jones came home from work while we were still sitting there. She waved like it was the most natural thing in the world to see us sitting on her lawn watching the cars.

Things really got busy around a quarter to five. We decided that the perfect spot was about fifteen feet from the corner. We didn't have to mark it; there was a fire hydrant on the other side that we could use as a marker.

When my mother drove down the street, she too waved at us like it was the most natural place to find me and my friends. Maybe doing what's right just feels like the most natural thing.

CHAPTER THIRTEEN

Maybe I was feeling *too* good. When the traffic started to die down and the twins said they were leaving, we stood up, still talking but moving toward our good-byes. We'd noticed how some of the cars slowed down and somebody inside would point at my house. Plank is a small town, and the KKK incident was in the newspaper and on television. So I didn't think too much of it when a car with three teenage boys inside slowed down to look at our house. What did shock me was when one of the boys, a lanky, clean-cut-looking white boy, hung out the window to shout the *N* word at us.

My immediate thought was my sister. I looked over at her group. All four of them were staring wide-eyed at the car as it passed. I started moving toward them, but they all took off running into my house. I figured that was the best place for them.

I turned and walked back to the twins. I couldn't read their expressions.

"I guess we know what to say now when we want to get rid of your sister and her friends," Jury said, smiling.

For the first time in a while, I wanted to hit him. "How can you make a joke about this?" I shouted. When all he did was smile and shrug, I lost it. I lunged toward him, but was intercepted by Judge, who caught me.

"Chill, Tommy," Judge said.

"Did you hear what they said?" I yelled. How could they be so calm?

"We heard."

Judge let go of me. Jury still hadn't said anything; he was staring at me like he'd seen a ghost. I took a deep breath. "Jury, I'm—"

"No problem, man." He held up his palm and I slapped it.

He looked at Judge, grinning. "Way to watch your bro's back." As he threw up his palm again, Judge reluctantly slapped it.

"My brother doesn't know when to stop, Tommy. I'd thought you'd know that by now."

"Sometimes laughter is the only medicine, guys," Jury said as they started toward their house. "I'm not going to let a couple of jerks get to me."

When I went inside, Quinn and her friends were helping my mother stuff envelopes. She was talking to them about intolerance. I know that was the word of the hour because all four of the girls used it in the short time it took for me to get a banana and a handful of cheese crackers.

"Why were you and the twins sitting on the curb like that, Tommy?" my mother asked.

"Just hanging out."

"Umph," she mumbled.

I don't know what she meant by that, but sometimes I think she can read my mind and she knows when I'm lying. I know parents set kids up to believe that, but she's been very convincing over the years.

"Is it okay if Judge and Jury stay over Saturday night?" I asked.

She looked up at the ceiling like that's where she keeps her calendar. "I guess so. Why, what are you planning?"

"Nothing. I figure we'll rent some movies."

"I want to see the titles before you watch them."

I grinned. "Why, don't you trust me?"

"I trust you. I trust you to act like a soon-to-be thirteen-year-old boy. Show me the titles."

"No problem." I went upstairs. Grinning at her like I had, I'm sure I made her think that any mischief we were planning had to do with movies. Parents have their tricks, but we have ours too.

My mother spent the rest of the evening on the telephone, so I wasn't able to call Angela to see if she and Faye had made the guides. I still wondered if we were really going to be able to pull this off.

I got my chance to talk to Angela first thing Friday morning. She called me before she left to walk to school. We met at the corner. When we were younger, we all used to coordinate our morning walks, but we haven't done it consistently since fourth grade.

She was smiling as she approached me. "So you've become part of that ever-growing group that wants to bash in Jury's big mouth?"

I felt the blood rush to my face. "I'm not real proud of that. Who told you?"

"Faye."

"Faye? Who told her?"

"Jury. He was laughing about it."

"He would."

We walked a few feet in silence. "So what's eating you, Tommy? Is it still the Vincent Chin rally?"

"It is and it isn't."

"That narrows things down for me, Tommy." She smiled and touched my shoulder.

My friendship with Angela has always been . . . what? More special than my friendship with the rest of the Posse. Angela puts her all into everything she does or cares about. She respects people who can do the same. She thinks *I'm* like that too. I'm not sure if I am, but I try to act like I am when I'm around her, because I like the respect I see in her eyes.

"Tommy, when I was in the fourth grade I discovered something. It was such an important discovery I talked to my father about it. He said he was very proud of me, because according to him, what I discovered most people don't discover until they're too old to enjoy the information."

"What was it?"

"I was at church, it was Christmastime. My Sunday school teacher wanted me to be the Virgin Mary in the Christmas pageant. She was going on and on about how this part had the most lines and how it would be difficult for some of the older students, but that she was sure I could handle it. She gave me the play book, in front of my parents, and she started telling us about when the rehearsals were and all that. But she never asked me if I wanted to do it. My mother was proud and starting talking about the outfit she was going to make for me and the Joseph character. My father noticed my expression and asked me what was wrong."

"What was wrong?"

"I handed the play book back to my Sunday school teacher. Then I told her that I was glad she thought I could do it, but I didn't *want* to do it. I explained that I was in a Christmas play at school and I was working on my science fair project and some of the other things I had coming up. I explained I just didn't have the time to take on another new project. What I discovered was, even as a kid, you don't have to do everything other people ask of you. Sometimes it's okay to say no. Tommy, if you don't want to participate in the Vincent Chin rally or even make the speed bump, don't. It's up to you—life will go on."

I tried to think of something to say, some way to explain to Angela how trapped I was feeling about this rally, but I couldn't. She was right. My mother is the best. Angela was absolutely right; I could tell her that I didn't want to participate in her rally and she would understand. That wasn't the problem. My problem was I didn't want her or anyone else to participate in it either. I just wanted to make the whole thing go away.

CHAPTER FOURTEEN

Friday was an interesting day. The counselors from the middle school were on campus. There were three of them and they met individually with each of the sixth-graders. By our lunch hour everybody was hyped about next year, about going to a school that had choices. Kids were talking about it as if they were going off to college and really had a choice of classes, but that's not what I got from my interview. The counselor said there would be six class periods each day and one period would be an elective. There was a list of nine elective classes, but some of them were offered only during certain semesters—like tennis, which was offered only in the spring. It was interesting to me, because some students were hearing only what they wanted to hear—"When you go to middle school, you get a choice of classes." I heard kids saying that they were planning to take six periods of gym! I guess they'd learn soon enough that choice didn't mean unrestricted freedom.

"We're at the beginning of the end," Faye said as we all sat at our usual lunch table.

"What do you mean?" Judge asked.

"You know how everybody gets during the last period of a school day? Especially a Friday, when the weather is really good and it's daylight saving time and a nice breeze is coming through the window?"

We all nodded.

"You can't quite pay attention to what the teacher's saying? If you're sitting near the window you want to see the plane that you can hear going overhead?"

"Yeah, I know what you mean," Jury said. "You feel like a caged animal."

"Right. That's what's going to be in the air from now until graduation."

Faye was right. For the next six weeks of school, we were going to be surrounded by "caged animals."

We all looked at each other. Faye, ever the romantic, was once again doing her running commentary on, as Jury says, the days of our lives. Faye just smiled and went back to eating her food, but the rest of the Posse looked as bummed out by her comment as I was feeling.

"Do you think we'll always be friends?" Angela asked.

"I don't see why not," Judge answered. "My mother and father have been friends since elementary school." I expected Jury to joke that even though his parents grew up together and their families were close, they were divorced, but he didn't.

When I thought about it, I realized that not only was it unnecessary information, but the divorce hadn't seemed to stop the friendship between his parents or their families. Judge's reminder that his parents have been friends forever seemed to improve everybody's mood. Before long, Jury was looking around the lunchroom, gearing up for the lunchtime pom-pom tackle game.

I was aware of the "caged animal effect" the rest of the day. By the time the dismissal bell rang, I felt sorry for Miss Hoffer. The poor woman looked exhausted. All afternoon she'd been telling us to "calm down"—"There's a little too much noise in the back"—and telling the next reader where we were in the book. I didn't add to her misery, but I have to admit, my mind hadn't been on my work. I was thinking about the speed bump, wondering if we were going to be able to pull this thing off.

After school, I met the twins at Angela's house. They went to their house first to get the wagon. The three of us took turns pulling the wooden guides that Angela and Faye had nailed together back to my house. It wasn't heavy, not at all. The only reason we took turns pulling it was because none of us wanted to be seen pulling a wagon around the neighborhood. We all have reputations to protect.

Just as we had hidden the wood away with the bag of

mortar, Faye's mother's car pulled up. Faye jumped out and got a new plastic trash can out of the trunk.

"What did you tell her?" I asked Faye as we added it to the rest of the stuff in the garage.

"I told her it was for a special project we're working on. So far she hasn't asked for any more details. I haven't got a clue as to what to tell her, but I'm hoping I can come up with something on the spot. I hate to lie to her. I'm figuring when the bump is discovered, I'll just tell her the truth."

"Really?"

"Yeah, I told you. My parents think we don't use the power we have. They'll probably think this is a good thing."

As the twins and I waved good-bye to Faye and her mother, I wondered if Faye was right. It's one thing to tell some kids you think they should be more active in their community. It's another thing to support them once they get in big trouble for it. That thought made me remember what my father had told me about publicity.

CHAPTER FIFTEEN

When I checked the clock, it was a few minutes to five. I got the telephone and called information. My parents always tell me to use the telephone book, since there's a charge for information, but I was in a hurry. I called Channel Four's news department and got the number I was looking for. Okay, I told myself when I finished, if there's any chance that my father can feel the kind of pride Faye believes her parents feel when she takes a stand, this will be his opportunity. Both of my parents went to a rally meeting that night. I couldn't believe I was hearing myself say it, but I told Quinn that I was getting sick of pizza for dinner.

The next morning started out strange. My father went to the hospital—that's pretty normal—but by the time I came downstairs, there were seven women in our family room. It was nine o'clock in the morning and these women looked like they'd been there for hours. What really surprised me was that my mother wasn't one of them. It's a good thing I got fully dressed before I came down. It's odd enough just to find seven extra people in your house first thing in the morning, but it was even stranger that I hadn't heard them. I wanted to ask them where my mother was, but they were already treating me like a baby ("Oh, look how tall he's gotten" and, "I bet you want to be a doctor too") and I didn't want to stand there asking, "Where's my mommy?" When I heard noises in the backyard, I excused myself to see what was going on.

The first thing I noticed when I looked out the back door was a pile of wood that looked just like the two long planks Faye and Angela put together for us. My heart jumped.

"Good morning, sweetie." It was my mom's voice, but I still couldn't see her. I stepped all the way outside. She was standing on the other side of the tree. There were two other women out there with her. I could see what they were doing—making signs.

My mother was smiling. She had her long hair pulled back in a ponytail and was wearing jeans and a University of Kentucky sweatshirt. I'd never noticed before how much alike she and Quinn look. With her cheeks red from the fresh air and activity, she looked like Quinn's teenage sister. She seemed so happy, I almost wanted to take her picture.

"What are you doing?" I asked, as if it wasn't obvious.

"This is our last weekend before the rally. Today we're making all the signs."

I wondered how this would affect what the Posse had planned for later. "So you guys will be around all day?"

"No, I'm going to meet with the college kids as soon as we finish here. In fact, I won't be around much at all today, so watch out for your sister."

"The twins can still spend the night, right?" Her look told me she'd forgotten.

"I guess it's still okay. Why don't you tell them that I'll pick them up at around six, and then I'll take the three of you to the video store. Maybe we can pick up some pizzas too." She grinned at me, then looked quizzical. "Why the big frown?"

"Believe it or not, I'm getting tired of pizza. I was hoping you would make paper-wrapped chicken for us."

She touched my forehead like she was checking for a temperature. "You're kidding, right?"

"No, I like your paper-wrapped chicken..."

"I know, honey, but it takes so long. I'd have to drive over to the Asian market; I need sesame oil and oyster sauce."

"Never mind. It was just a thought."

"I'll make it for you next Sunday, after the rally. I promise. But if you're getting tired of pizza, I can get some other kind of takeout."

"Okay." I knew there was a good chance I'd already said too much about it. My mother has this image of what a good mother does and she'll worry if she thinks she's falling short. "It's no big deal, Mom, really."

There was a wrinkle in the middle of her forehead. I know her, paper-wrapped chicken was going to be in the back of her mind all day. There was no way to fix it. Any more talk about food was bound to make matters worse.

I glanced in the garage before I went back inside. Thankfully, the speed bump stuff was still hidden in the corner.

Quinn was in the kitchen eating when I went back into the house. "Good morning, squirt," I said. She's becoming a real master with that ponytail device. The style she was wearing today looked like something women would have to pay somebody to do.

"How does my hair look?"

I studied it like I hadn't noticed it until just then. "It's all right."

She grinned. "It's fantastic and you know it."

"Let me get this right. I'm supposed to care about your silly ponytails?"

"You're such a boy."

That surprised me. It sounded like something Faye or Angela would say. "Is that supposed to be criticism?"

She jerked her head around, turning her back on me like she thought I was hopeless. I fought the urge to hug her. It's so weird to see her growing up before my eyes. I remember when they brought her home from the hospital. My father's car was packed with gifts and most of the boxes had something inside for me too. I've always liked having this little girl around.

"Do you have any plans for today?" I asked her.

She smiled like she wanted to say something cute, but thought better of it. "Not really. Do you want to go to the movies?"

"Maybe. Judge and Jury are planning to spend the night. I need to find out what time they're coming over."

"Do you think they get tired of always being called Judge and Jury?"

"What do you mean? Those're their names."

She gave me her impatient look again. "I get tired of people saying Tommy and Quinn, and I'm sure I don't hear it as often as they hear 'Judge and Jury.' Have you ever thought about reversing the order?"

"No, but I will."

"Tommy?"

"No, Quinn!" I knew she was getting ready to ask me one of her silly riddles.

"Just one?"

"Okay, what?"

"Where do books sleep?"

"I don't know, where?"

"Under their covers, of course." She was grinning as I walked away.

Jury and Judge, it sounded weird that way, but I promised myself I would try it for a while. It's funny too, because Judge is not the twin most people would think of first. Jury has the strongest personality—definitely the alpha male.

I went back upstairs and started separating clothes to wash. My mother stopped doing my laundry for me last year. She said she didn't want to rob me of the opportunity to take care of myself. She said it with a straight face too. I don't mind doing my own washing; at least I always know what's clean now.

"Honey, will you be a dear and wash a towel load too?"

I jumped—I thought my mother was still outside. Sometimes she moves like a cat.

"With so many friends around, we're running through towels like a gym."

"No problem," I told her. I was surprised when she came into my room.

"Well, Tommy, it's just about over. This time next week we'll be at the rally." She looked at me carefully. "I hope all the attention hasn't been too hard on you and Quinn."

"We're okay."

She smiled. "Yes, you are." And then she was gone. She moves in a way that can make you question whether or not she was actually there. It's silly to think about it now, but when I was a little kid, I used to think she floated into my room at night; I could always hear my dad coming, but never her. I took my load of whites downstairs and then returned for the towels. I finally called the twins while my last load was drying.

Judge was at the library, but Jury said they'd be ready

whenever we got there to pick them up. I tried not to let her see me, but I checked on Quinn again. She was still sitting on Latecia's steps. They seemed to be playing with their Barbie dolls, but I couldn't tell for sure without going all the way outside.

It looked like we weren't going to make it to the movies. That's the thing about washing clothes, it always takes longer than you'd expect. It was almost one o'clock when I finished and decided to eat lunch. The good thing about having a bunch of extra women around is they travel with dishes—at least my mother's friends do. There were three unfamiliar bowls in the refrigerator. I decided to eat from the one that looked like a taco salad.

It looked like Quinn had been in to eat too. I couldn't tell what she had, but there was a plate and glass on the counter. I ate standing over the sink, looking out the window at the street. Two cars passed, both of them moving slowly. We wouldn't have a problem if our workweek traffic was as slow as the weekend traffic. I thought about my mother's rally. If life was perfect, there wouldn't be a need for any form of protest. But life wasn't perfect.

CHAPTER SIXTEEN

Considering that my mind was racing with thoughts about our plan, the day was fairly normal. My mother came back a little after three. I was in the family room listening to music videos.

"Has your dad called?"

"Yup. He said he'll be back before five. He went to—"

"I know, hit a few balls."

I laughed. "Those were his exact words. Mrs. Jones took Quinn and Latecia to the movies. I hope that was okay?"

"Fine. What were they going to see?"

"I didn't ask."

"I'm sure Brenda would've checked." She was standing in the kitchen going through the mail. "What time do you want to pick up the twins?"

"In a few hours." I thought about what Quinn had said. "Mom, do you think Judge and Jury get tired of being called Judge and Jury?"

She put the mail back on the table. "As opposed to what, baby?"

"Jury and Judge."

"Oh." She seemed to be thinking about it. "I'm sure they do, at least Jury probably does. I get tired of hearing people say 'The doctor and Mrs.'" She walked over and sat down next to me. "You know Dr. Woodruff, at the hospital?"

I nodded to let her know I knew whom she was talking about.

"One time she told me that people get so confused about how to address her and her husband as a couple, they just ignore the fact that she's a doctor. She said most of their invitations read Mr. and Mrs."

"How would you do it, since she doesn't use his last name?"

"I'm not sure; I'd have to look it up, but I guess it's Mr. James Locke and Dr. Sherry Woodruff."

I nodded. "Yeah, sometimes the logical way is the easiest."

She patted my leg. "*Most* of the time the logical way is the easiest way." She got up and left the room.

I thought about the speed bump. It was the logical answer to a problem; at least it sounded like it at the time.

Angela called to go through the final checklist with me. I knew it was killing her not to be in on the actual making of the bump. Angela loves to see a good plan come together.

"Have you decided what you're going to do next weekend?" she asked just before we hung up.

"What do you mean?"

"Are you going to give your mother your support at the rally?" She exhaled loudly, like there shouldn't have been a need to explain.

"It's not a matter of supporting my mother."

"Then what is it?"

I tried to find the words. "It's about being on display, Angela."

"Tommy, it's like they used to say—you're either part of the solution or part of the problem. You can't have it both ways."

"You're thinking like Faye and sounding like Jury."

"Yeah, well sometimes even Faye and Jury are right," she said. "I'll be over there tomorrow, as soon as I get out of church."

"Okay, 'bye," I said.

I was in my bedroom, straightening it up, when my mother found me at about a quarter to five.

"We better leave, so we can get back before Quinn returns."

My heart jumped, and I knew it wasn't out of excitement about seeing my friends.

Jury and Judge seemed to be as nervous as I was. Judge talked too much and Jury was quiet. In other words, they had reversed personalities. As soon as they got in the car, Judge started questioning my mother about her new favorite subject.

"How many people are you expecting at the rally?" he asked her.

"There's no way to tell. Three buses are leaving from the college here, so it should be a good crowd. The students at Kentucky State have really embraced it too. With them being right there in Frankfort, they've handled a lot of the business for us. We couldn't have gotten this far without them."

Judge smiled. Kentucky State is one of the historically black colleges. He seemed to take pride in what my mother had just told him. I looked at Jury; he was smiling too.

We chose three videos, which I knew was a mistake. In my family, we never get to watch all of the second video before everybody falls asleep. After the video store, we went to the deli and got submarine sandwiches. My mother told the twins we had a refrigerator full of salads.

My father and Quinn were home when we got there. Daddy was in the shower and Quinn was half asleep in front of the television. She perked up when she saw the twins.

"Hi Jury and Judge," she said, looking at me with a knowing grin. The guys looked at me to explain the joke. I just shrugged like I didn't know. It would have taken too much effort to explain.

Quinn didn't waste any time in telling the twins her latest jokes. When my father came downstairs he challenged them to beat him at his latest video game. It's always like that when they visit. Between my sister fawning all over them and my father testing his video skills, I feel like I have to make an appointment. Sometimes I wish I enjoyed video games as much as they do. I play them, but I can't sit there for hours at it. And, to me, watching a game being played is the definition of boring. I've promised myself that I'm going to take an interest in golf during summer vacation. That will make my father happy. Too bad I can't get him interested in pom-pom tackle.

The sun was starting to go down by the time we finished dinner.

"Do we have time for one quick basketball game?" I asked my mother.

"In the driveway?" she asked. I got the impression she was still trying to figure out what we were up to. Maybe she thought it was a trick question.

"Uh huh, right in our driveway."

"Go ahead. Don't let it get too dark before you come in."

"No problem."

Like most of the homes in our neighborhood, our garage is a separate building behind our house. Faye lives in a new part of town and her garage is attached to the house. Sometimes when it's really cold out and my mother sends me out to the garage, I envy Faye's setup, but this wasn't one of those days.

The net is attached to the garage. We actually shot a few baskets when we went out. After about ten minutes, which I figured was long enough to get my parents used to the sound of the bouncing ball, I started telling the guys the plan.

I bounced the ball while we talked. "Okay, one of us will need to keep up the basketball noise at all times." They nodded. "I guess we need to mix the mortar now. I figure if we add a little more water than needed, it'll be just right by the time we need to use it."

"What about the water?" Jury asked. "Won't we have to go inside to get it?"

It was too early in the year for the hose to be out, but that wasn't a problem.

"No, we can use the faucet over there." I pointed to the connection that was under the family room window. "But I don't think we should bother with connecting the hose. There should be something in the garage we can use to carry the water."

I tossed the ball to Judge and he started shooting baskets. Jury and I went into the garage. I showed him the trash can Faye brought over. We lifted the bag of mortar and put it in the clean trash can. I found a bleach bottle that my father had cut the top off of. I don't know what he used it for, but it was perfect for carrying water. I filled it up three times and poured the water over the dry mortar. We used a yard-stick to stir it. "One more container of water should make it just a little runny," I told Jury.

"Don't forget about me," Judge said as I passed with the water.

I told Jury that it was time to change places with his brother. He looked like he wanted to protest, but he didn't. I heard them arguing, but most of the time if they're talking, they're arguing. It was funny to me. They were out there arguing about who was going to be "forced" to play basketball.

Judge and I got the mixture at the consistency that we thought would keep. Remembering back to my sister's mud-pie days, I would say the mixture was just a little too runny to hold its shape. I was betting that in a few hours it would be perfect.

"I figure we should get out here a few times to stir it before the night's over."

"How will we explain that?" Judge asked.

"I have no idea."

CHAPTER SEVENTEEN

On a typical movie night, my mother will be in her room sewing or reading and my father will be on his computer. This time, both of them sat in the family room with us and watched the first movie. It wasn't even the type of movie my mother usually watches; she doesn't like science fiction. Quinn was the only one acting normal—she fell asleep leaning against our father.

When the movie was over, he woke her and helped her upstairs. I expected my mother to follow, but she didn't. She watched all the previews on the second video. Just before the movie started, I went into the kitchen to get a soda.

"Do you want me to take the garbage out?" I asked her when I returned.

She looked at me like I was speaking the alien language featured in the first movie.

"No, it can wait until the morning."

"I don't mind. I can smell it."

"I'll go out with you," Jury volunteered. "I'll watch his back, Mrs. M," he said to my confused mother.

We went to the kitchen before she had a chance to think about it. I turned on the floodlights that are on the side of the house.

"I'll watch his back, Mrs. M," I mimicked.

"Hey, I had to say something."

Jury went in to stir the mixture while I put the trash in the can. I peeked into the garage. "Is it soup yet?" I don't know why that struck him as so funny, but he cracked up. "Quiet, my mother might hear you." Then he started. It was late and we were punchy. The next thing I knew, Judge was coming out the back door.

"Your mother said to stop all that noise. She said this ain't no residential area, folks live up in here!"

I didn't even know then that he was doing a line from one of his grandfather's old Richard Pryor albums. I just knew it was something my mother would never say, and it was funny. I laughed with them. "Okay guys, we're too close to blow it now. We better go in," I finally said.

It wasn't a moment too soon. We found my mother putting on her sweater.

"Tommy, it's too late for you guys to be out there making all that noise."

"I know, we're sorry."

She looked at us. We were all grinning. I'm sure we didn't look sorry.

"I'm going to bed. Try to make it upstairs before daybreak. Good night, boys."

"Good night," we said in unison.

I knew her "mother radar" had to have been running in overdrive. She knew we were up to something, but apparently she couldn't wait it out. She didn't go right up; she never does after she says good night. We heard her in the kitchen, probably taking food out of the freezer for Sunday's meal. To me, mothers remembering to do stuff like that is fascinating. Knowing her, she'd figured out what to cook on Sunday and what part of it would still be around for lunches on Monday. We heard her going upstairs about twenty minutes after she said good night.

"Now what?" Judge asked. "Do we go out and make the bump now or stick to the original plan?"

The original plan was to go to sleep, but set the alarm to get up around three. "I think we should stick to the plan. If we do it now, we could be seen," I told them. It was 12:33. Early enough for some of the neighbors to still be awake, although I couldn't imagine which ones. They all strike me as early-to-bed types.

"So we're going up?" Judge asked.

"Yeah, let's give my mom a few more minutes. Usually she reads before she falls asleep."

We watched the first half of the second movie. It was one the three of us had already seen in the theater, so I don't know why we rented it. It wasn't very good the first time. Finally, when I couldn't stand the wait any longer, I made my announcement: "Let's go up."

I closed up the house like a man with a mission. I tried to make sure there was nothing on the floor for one of us to trip over at three in the morning. Since we didn't want to talk or turn on the television for fear we would wake somebody, there was nothing left to do but go to sleep. I didn't think I'd be able to sleep, so the alarm clock ringing under my pillow came as quite a surprise.

I was afraid to turn on the light, but I had to. Jury was asleep on a chair that folds out to the size of a twin mattress, and I didn't want to step on him. Judge was asleep in the other bunk bed. I already knew from past experience that they're hard people to wake, especially Judge. I shook Jury first. He mumbled something and rolled over. I shook him again and he said, "You go first, Judge."

I wasn't sure what that meant, so I shook him again. He said "you go first" again. I leaned down close to his ear. "I'm finished," I said. I figured that whatever Judge was supposed to do first, Jury was set to get up and do it second. His eyes popped open as he was saying "No, you didn't." He stopped and looked at me. I didn't have on my glasses, but that wasn't enough to make me look like his brother.

We got to the garage without the twins arguing or trying to kill each other. We couldn't turn on the floodlight—that thing throws off enough light to wake up my ancestors. I brought a flashlight. We had to make two trips to the garage. The mortar had become very heavy; it took two of us to carry the trash can.

On the second trip, the twins carried the wood and I carried a shovel. The street was dead quiet. There were all kinds of strange animal sounds; something that sounded like a cat and maybe an owl or two. A couple of dogs were barking in the distance.

We lined the wood up using the fire hydrant marker. There was a lot of discussion about whether or not the guide boards were straight. Luckily the street was wide. There would be no reason for anybody to drive over the bump until it was set. We took turns shoveling the mortar between the guide boards. That was the hardest part. It had thickened up a lot. The fun part was smoothing out the bump. I brought two pairs of rubber gloves and all three of us wanted to do the smoothing part. I gave the twins the gloves and went back to get some water. The water helped us smooth out the bump. The whole process took all of thirty minutes. Considering we were just kids, we worked remarkably well and fast together. The next problem didn't come until we were finished. We had to decide whether or not to remove the guide boards.

"It'll set better if we leave them," Jury said.

"*Duh,*" Judge said, which was odd, because I know he hates that expression.

"The point is, we won't be able to get them back before everybody gets up."

They looked at me. "Maybe," I said, making up what I wanted to say as I went along. "Maybe that's a good thing."

"Why?" one of them said.

"Because we don't have anywhere to hide them and, if somebody finds the boards, they'll know we made the bump." Nobody said anything for a few minutes, maybe it was a few seconds, but time moves slowly when you're standing in the middle of the street at three in the morning.

"Yeah, plus any Sunday driver will be moving slow enough to see them and drive around, giving the bump time to dry," said Jury.

It was decided. We all turned back to give one final look at our masterpiece. I didn't know what was going to happen, but I was proud.

We rinsed out the plastic trash can and hid it in the garage. Everything was moving well until we got to the top of the stairs and heard the toilet flush.

We froze.

Both of the bathrooms upstairs are connected to bedrooms. There's a bathroom off of my parents' bedroom and one in between mine and Quinn's room. There was no reason for anybody to come out into the hallway, *unless* they decided to go downstairs for a snack. It had to be close to four in the morning. Sometimes my mother gets up very early. I can't tell you what she does during those times because I try to stay in bed until the last possible moment. When it had been quiet for several minutes, I decided the early-morning wanderer was Quinn and that she had gone back to bed. We tiptoed back to my room. I was too hyped to fall right asleep, but the twins didn't seem to have any trouble.

A knock at my door woke me.

"Tommy? Tommy, are you up?"

It was Quinn, speaking in her sweet little sister's voice.

Lately she's been acting so old and smart; I haven't heard her "Tommy will you help me?" voice in months—well, with the exception of the Latecia incident. I stepped over one of the twins and opened the door.

"Tommy, you guys have to get dressed and get outside!"

"Why?"

"Something wonderful has happened."

"What time is it?"

Her "adult" face came back. That wasn't the right question. I should have asked her what wonderful thing.

"It's almost ten. You've got to get the twins and get dressed."

I stepped all the way out of my room and into the hallway. I gently closed the door behind me, but I doubt if regular conversation would have been enough to wake them.

"This better not be about some silly joke, Quinn." That confused her enough to cancel my first wrong response. She studied me for a moment before she spoke again.

"It's not a joke. There's a speed bump in the middle of the street!"

My reaction was going to be important. "A what?"

"A speed bump. Last night somebody put a speed bump down. The wood is still there and everything."

I scrunched up my face like I was thinking. "Oh, I know what you mean. Like those bumps on the college campus?"

Her eyes twinkled. "Right! You've got to come see it!"

"Okay, but that's really odd. I didn't know the city worked on Sunday mornings."

"Tommy, you don't understand! The city didn't do it. It's a homemade speed bump."

I let a look of shock sweep my face. It must have been convincing, since she was on the verge of jumping up and down with delight. I told Quinn we would be right out. She walked away with a look of satisfaction on her face.

I woke the guys. "We better get out there or somebody is going to wonder why we're so sleepy," I said.

I got the bathroom first; I told them I had something I had to do before we went out. Luckily both of my parents were out front when I got downstairs. I went to my dad's office. The note that I wanted to fax was already written. I'd taken care of it on Friday, right after I called to get the fax number. After I'd written and printed out the letter, I'd hidden it in one of my father's medical books. I turned on his machine and fed it the note. The first time I put it in backward, so I had to redo it. I hope what my father had said about publicity was going to work for us. When I got back upstairs the twins were ready. Judge was making some noise about being hungry, but we overruled him. Breakfast could wait until after we'd checked out the mysterious new bump.

CHAPTER EIGHTEEN

By the time we got out front, a few neighbors were still standing around talking. My mother was in a discussion with two women. Quinn was playing with the three-year-old who lives a few houses down. I don't know where my father was. Nobody was paying any attention to our speed bump and that bothered me. Okay, it didn't look nearly as impressive in daylight as it had in the dark. Somebody had removed the wood guides, and it looked smaller than I thought we had made it, but surely it deserved more attention than the neighbors were giving it.

"It looks kind of sad and puny, doesn't it?" Jury said as the three of us stood over it like it was somebody's grave.

"And not as smooth as I thought it would be," Judge added.

I felt like I had to say something to lift their spirits. "It'll slow them down, and that's what's important."

"Tommy's right, in the land of the blind, the one-eyed man is king. And the bottom line is if three guys our age could make one in a half hour in total darkness, the city has no excuse, with all its manpower and resources."

Jury slapped me on the back. I looked around. It wouldn't do for somebody to see him congratulating me. Thankfully, nobody, not a soul, was watching us.

"Now what?" Judge asked.

"If things go like I planned, our bump should be getting some attention real soon," I said. "But meanwhile, let's go shoot some baskets."

"Or get something to eat?" Judge asked.

We went back to the house. Judge ate a bowl of cereal. Jury and I each drank a glass of orange juice, and I caught him picking the corner off one of the sweet rolls my mother left out for us. After that, we went out to shoot some baskets. The guys weren't in any hurry to get home. They wanted to wait until they were sure their mother had gone to church. They wanted to avoid going themselves, and the chores their mother would have assigned if she'd known they were staying home.

Suddenly Quinn, apparently the new town crier, came running into the middle of our game. If she was hollering her usual "Tom-*mee!*" I was too caught up in the game to hear.

"The news van is looking at the bump!"

"Vans can't look at bumps," I joked.

"Tom-*mee*!"

Unlike for me, the news team was news to the twins. They walked to the edge of the driveway.

"She's right, the news van *is* here."

"Foxy Four?"

"I don't see her."

Jury turned to me. "You did this, didn't you?"

I nodded.

"Cool," Judge said. The three of us watched the cameraman as he pointed the big video camera at our bump.

"Let's go over and hear what they're saying," I said.

Someone had put a red flag on a pole in front of the bump. My father was approaching us, walking from the backyard of one of the neighbors.

"Tommy, do you guys know anything about this bump?" he asked. I put my right hand in my pocket and crossed my fingers. "Just what Quinn told us," I lied. That wouldn't have been enough for my mother, but it was for my dad. He was already back in conversation with Mr. Reynolds.

The on-air person was talking to a group of kids. They were telling him about how fast the cars come down the street on weekdays. He was trying to get one of them to say who they believed made the bump. The kids didn't seem to care about that question. Obviously they thought it was a good idea no matter what.

"My friend Latecia, she's at church, almost got hit by a car last week," Quinn volunteered. "And she's deaf!"

I got as close as I could. "Things should get real interesting around four-thirty tomorrow," I said, as loud as necessary. I could almost see the little wheels turning in the man's head. He wrapped up what he was saying, but he told the crowd that he would be back on Monday.

Not too long after the van left, Angela came over. She was duly impressed. "Not bad at all guys," she said as she examined it. "The red flag is a nice touch too."

I noticed that Judge started to say something, but Jury stopped him. He was probably going to tell her that the red flag hadn't been our idea. We decided to go see a movie and that was pretty much the end of the bump story for Sunday.

The day was so long at school on Monday that it felt like the last day before vacation. I wasn't suffering from the caged-animal effect, but I was very anxious to get home to see what would happen with the afterwork traffic.

After school I learned that everybody in the Posse had been as excited as I was. Without a lot of discussion about "playing a quick game of pom-pom tackle," or looking for one member or another, all five of us were ready to walk to my house immediately after class. It was fun walking home. Lately, it's been hard to get all of us together after school. It reminded me of what it was like when we were little kids and before Faye's family moved. This time the crowd on my street didn't concern me. The news van was there, but it was parked in one of the neighbors' driveways. I guess they didn't want any of the drivers to see it and slow down before they got to the bump. There was a car, with the city seal on its side, parked in front of Latecia's house.

"It's Foxy Four!" Jury said as he picked up speed walking down the hill.

As fast as Jury was walking, he didn't reach the bump as fast as Quinn reached us.

"Tommy, guys, the newspeople are back!" she said excitedly. Then she spotted Jury and started shouting, "I've got a joke!" Jury is Quinn's special joke friend. I like the way my friends treat my sister. One time Angela called to talk to me and Quinn answered the telephone. Angela must have heard something in Quinn's voice and asked her what was wrong. Quinn told Angela her problem—I don't remember now what it was, but that's not the point. They talked for so long, I was shocked when Quinn handed me the phone. I figured she'd been talking to one of her friends. When I found out it was Angela, I told her thanks for being nice to my sister.

"I like Quinn. Anyway, we're just following your lead, Tommy. If you treated her like she was a little pest, we probably would too. Look at how the guys treat Wayne's little brother." Wayne DeVoe is one of our classmates. He has a bunch of brothers and sisters. He's not very nice to them, but Wayne's not very nice to anybody.

"It better be good, squirt. That's Foxy Four down there," Jury told her.

Everybody stopped to hear the joke.

"Knock, knock."

"Who's there?" all of us said at the same time.

"The impatient cow."

"The impa—"

"Mooooo," she interrupted, then fell down laughing. Jury gave her a high five. All of us cracked up.

I don't know how Jury was able to spot Foxy Four. By the time we got to the bump I could see that she was holding up traffic at the other corner. Quinn told us she was asking drivers what they thought of the bump.

"Like somebody's going to admit that they hate it!" Faye said.

"Right," Jury agreed. "I hate it, Miss Scott, I usually do sixty-five on this street," Jury said, doing his stiff old-guy imitation.

Jury gave up on trying to get Mariama Scott's attention. We walked back up the street and sat down on Latecia's lawn. The majority of the cars slowed down and went around the bump. Most of the rest went over it gently. A few weren't paying any attention to all the clues around them and came ripping down the hill as usual. They were the fun ones to watch. The bump was just big and unexpected enough to cause some very funny expressions on the drivers' faces. It's a good thing the weather wasn't hot or their windows would have been down and little kids would've heard some of their verbal reactions.

I hate to say this, but the bump looked lopsided. I think somebody must have driven over it before it was completely dry. Angela and Faye questioned the guy from the city. He was an engineer from the department responsible for the speed bumps.

"Do you kids know who made it?" he asked.

"No, why? Is he or she in trouble?" Angela asked.

The city guy looked all around like he was about to pass government secrets. "Well, this bump is getting so much publicity, we'd probably be in trouble with the public if we tried to prosecute. We are going to break it up, but we'll put down a real one in its place. It turns out that whoever made this one put it in almost exactly the right spot."

After hearing that, I didn't think the day could get much better, but it did. Mrs. Jones came out of her house with a plate of homemade chocolate chip cookies.

"You're a good boy, Tommy, and you have good friends," she said as she winked at me. My heart jumped. She must have seen the fear on my face. She touched my arm. "Enjoy the cookies," she said.

Surprisingly enough, my mother didn't say anything to me about the speed bump until the following Friday night. We drove to the state capital Friday afternoon. It was exciting, because all four of us were together as a family at a time when we should have still been in school or at work. We were going to spend the night in a hotel, and that's always fun. I could tell my mother was pretty hyped about the rally. I hadn't said anything to her yet, but I'd finally come to my senses about it.

With the help of my friends, I'd begun to understand how important it is to do what you can to improve your life and the lives of the people you care about. I was planning to attend the rally and actually looking forward to it. I was proud of my mother and I was planning to tell her just before we got to the rally. I wanted her to know that my pride didn't have anything to do with the size of the crowd or any of that. I was proud of her effort.

When we got to the hotel, my father and Quinn left me and Mom in the room while they went out to buy snacks. I was watching television and my mother was writing at the desk.

At some point she came over and sat down next to me. "Tommy, before we left home, I noticed that we've mysteriously acquired a new trash can. Do you know anything about that?" She was grinning knowingly.

"No, it's a mystery to me," I said.

"I thought you'd say that." She tousled my hair the way she used to when I was a little kid. "Remember when we talked about my mother last week?"

I nodded.

"I guess I'll never know if she was a happy child. But I do believe that if she's looking down at her grandson, she's a proud and happy grandmother, Tomo-Kun."

"If she's looking at me, then she sees you too. She's a proud and happy mother, Mom."

AUTHOR'S NOTE

There are newsworthy events in young people's lives that change their perception of the world forever; these events are often called "defining moments." The assassination of President John F. Kennedy was that kind of event for young people of my generation. However, it's an unfortunate truth that such events tend to affect you less as you grow older. But every now and then something happens in the world that rocks an adult's soul in the same way it would have had he or she been much younger. The murder of Vincent Chin affected me that way.

I remember my initial thought was "How unfair." I learned in researching *A Day for Vincent Chin and Me* that his last words were "It's not fair." When I decided to have each member of the Posse tell his or her story, I knew Tommy would somehow want to tell his readers about Vincent Chin.

Vincent Chin did not die in vain. His brutal murder was

the spark that ignited and united Asians in this country. By 1982, many Asian Americans from Japan, China, and Korea had lived in this country for generations. Southeast Asians had been in the United States long enough to become united in their use of English, but it took the Vincent Chin case to make many Asian Americans realize that the majority population didn't recognize or acknowledge the differences in their separate cultures. Chinese Americans were then joined in protest by other Asian Americans, and many of today's organizations have formed from those alliances. It is my hope that this book can be part of the growing cultural awareness and education that has become Vincent Chin's legacy.

THE TRIALS OF VINCENT CHIN*

June 19, 1982 Vincent Chin attends his bachelor party at Fancy Pants, a club in suburban Detroit. Autoworkers Ronald Ebens and his stepson, Michael Nitz, enter the bar. Ebens taunts Chin, whom he mistakenly thinks is from Japan, which he blames for the ailing U.S. auto industry. A fight ensues. After the fight is broken up, Chin leaves the club. Twenty minutes later, Ebens and Nitz find Chin in front of a McDonald's. Ebens knocks Chin down and beats him with a baseball bat.

June 23, 1982 Vincent Chin dies as a result of his injuries.

March 16, 1983 Wayne County Judge Charles Kaufman finds Ebens and Nitz guilty of manslaughter after a plea

*Reprinted with permission from "Remembering Vincent Chin" by Alethea Yip, AsianWeek.com, June 5–13, 1997 (http://www.asianweek.com/061397/feature.html).

bargain and sentences each of them to three years' probation, a $3,000 fine, and $780 in court fees. The prosecuting attorney is not present and neither Chin's mother nor any witnesses are called to testify.

November 1983 The U.S. Justice Department, following an FBI investigation, files charges, and a federal grand jury indicts Ebens and Nitz on two counts—one for violating Chin's civil rights and the other for conspiracy.

June 1984 Ebens is found guilty of violating Chin's civil rights but not of conspiracy. He is sentenced to twenty-five years in prison but is released on a $20,000 bond. Nitz is cleared of both charges.

September 1986 Ebens's conviction is overturned by a federal appeals court on a legal technicality; an American Citizens for Justice attorney is accused of improperly coaching prosecution witnesses.

April 1987 Under intense public pressure, the Justice Department orders a retrial, but this time in a new venue: Cincinnati.

May 1987 The Cincinnati jury clears Ebens of all charges.

July 1987 A civil suit orders Ebens to pay $1.5 million to Chin's estate as part of a court-approved settlement. However, Ebens disposes of his assets and flees the state. He has not paid any of the settlement.

September 1987 Disgusted with the country's legal system, Lily Chin, Vincent Chin's mother, leaves the United States and moves back to her native village in Guangzhou, China.